GOALKEEPER
IN CHARGE

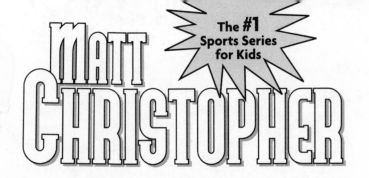

The #1
Sports Series
for Kids

GOALKEEPER IN CHARGE

Text by Robert Hirschfeld

Little, Brown and Company
Boston   New York   London

First Edition

Matt Christopher™ is a trademark of Catherine M. Christopher.

The characters and events in this book are fictitious. Any similarity to real
persons, living or dead, is coincidental and not intended by the author.

Text written by Robert Hirschfeld

ISBN 0-316-07552-3
LCCN 2002102952

10 9 8 7 6 5 4 3 2 1

MV-NY

Printed in the United States of America

You're such a DOPE! I can't believe how lame you are! I'm ashamed to know you!

Tina Esparza kicked a pebble off the sidewalk, as if the pebble had said those hurtful things to her. Of course, it hadn't said a thing.

A nasty little voice in Tina's own head had said them. And she knew she deserved every word.

She was walking home from school with her best friend, Meg Janis. Tina, slender and dark-haired, was a few inches shorter than Meg, whose hair was light brown and curly. The girls were twelve years old and this had been their second day of seventh grade. For Tina, it hadn't been a good day at all. In fact, it had been *terrible*.

What's the matter with you, anyway? the nasty little voice whined. Don't you have any sense at all?

"Tina?" asked Meg, looking at her friend with a puzzled expression. "Did you say something?" When Tina didn't reply, she spoke again, a little louder. "Hello? Anybody home? *HEY!*"

Startled, Tina blinked and looked at Meg. "Huh? Why are you yelling at me?"

Meg rolled her eyes. "I was yelling because you didn't seem to hear me when I talked in a regular voice. You were mumbling to yourself, and you looked like you'd swallowed a rotten egg. What's going on?"

Tina said, "Nothing's going on."

"Hey, Teen, this is Meg, remember? Your friend Meg? Don't say nothing's going on, because I know that there has to be something.

"It isn't just now, either. Today, when Ms. Gould asked you about the poem we read in class, about what it meant, remember? You just sat there like she was speaking some weird language you didn't understand. I know you're smart. I know you could've come up with an answer, but you just sat there. How come?"

Tina was tempted to say she didn't know what Meg was talking about, but Meg *was* her closest friend, and Tina knew that she had to talk to somebody. She sighed.

"Sure, I knew the answer," she admitted. "It's just that when she asked the question and the other kids turned to look at me and . . . I just felt all these eyes *staring* at me . . . and I . . . couldn't . . . *talk*. My brain wouldn't work, my mouth wouldn't work, and I, well, *you* know. It's not like it's the first time."

Meg nodded. "No, it's happened before. But I think it's getting worse lately. Am I right?"

"I don't know, I guess," answered Tina. "Ms. Gould must think I'm totally dumb. And when it happens in other classes, those teachers will think so too. I do the same thing when I'm with a bunch of other kids. It's like, sometimes I turn into a statue for a while. The worst part is, I don't have a clue what to do about it."

Meg thought it over. "I wouldn't worry about teachers. You do well on tests and homework, and they'll know you're smart. But the other kids . . . it won't make you Miss Popularity with other girls if you go around imitating a clam with its shell shut tight. And as for *boys* — well, forget it."

"I don't care about boys," Tina said.

3

"No?" Meg sounded doubtful. "Okay, if you say so. But you may change your mind someday."

The girls had reached Tina's house. "Want to kick a ball around for a while?" Tina asked. "We could use some practice." Both girls loved soccer and would start playing with a team called the Wildcats in a few days. The Wildcats were part of a league for players from twelve to fourteen. Now that they were twelve, their games would be on a full-sized field, with eleven players on each team.

"Sure," Meg agreed. "There isn't much homework yet, so I have time."

"Wait a second," Tina called, running to the garage to get a ball. She came out dribbling the ball, passing it from foot to foot. The girls went into Tina's backyard and began kicking the ball around the lawn.

"What's your favorite part of soccer?" Meg asked as she received Tina's pass with her knee and let the ball drop to the grass. "Shooting? Passing? Tough defense?"

Tina stopped Meg's kick by trapping the ball under her shoe. "My favorite?" She expertly flipped the ball up, juggled it from one knee to the other,

4

and kicked it back to Meg. "I guess my favorite part is that it's a team sport."

"Yeah, I know what you mean," Meg said, trying unsuccessfully to flip the ball up as Tina had done. Meg wasn't as good as Tina. She knew it and had no problem with it. "Teamwork, playing as a team, it's pretty cool."

"Actually," Tina said, "what I mean is, when there are a lot of players out there, nobody's watching *you*, especially. You know? You just sort of fit in with the group. That's what I really like. Now we'll have eleven on the same side, and it'll be even easier to just blend in."

Meg laughed. "You're strange sometimes. You're the only player I know who doesn't want to be a star. In fact, you'd *hate* it, because people *look* at stars. Am I right?"

Tina trapped the ball under her foot. "You're right," she agreed, and laughed. "I'd probably like it even better if there were *twenty* players on a team. Anyway, I hope I'll be able to keep doing the same things with the Wildcats that I'm used to doing."

Meg shook her head. "Weird," she said. "How did

I ever get to be friends with such a weird person? Oh, by the way, I heard some stuff about the Wildcats' coach. My cousin played for her last year."

"What did you hear?" asked Tina.

Meg said, "Well, her name is Danielle Barron. My cousin says she was fun to work with, that she never screamed at anyone, and that all she wants is for everyone to do her best. She isn't one of those 'We have to win, and nothing else matters' coaches."

"Sounds good," Tina said, getting her foot under the ball and chipping it high so that Meg could "head" it — hit the ball with her forehead. In soccer, you can touch the ball with any part of your body except your hands and arms, unless you're a goalkeeper. Goalkeepers, or keepers, can use their hands to catch and throw the ball.

Meg lunged at the ball, which bounced off the top of her head at a crazy angle and went into the bushes. As she turned to get it, a voice called out from nearby: "When you head the ball, try to hit it with the middle of your forehead, right below your hairline."

Tina and Meg turned and saw a boy of about their age standing at the back door of the neighboring

6

house. He had straw-blond hair and blue eyes, and had just moved into the neighborhood. Tina knew that Meg's big smile was a sign that Meg thought he was cute.

"Hi," Tina said. "You're Dave, right?"

The boy nodded. "Dave Knowles. You're Tina?"

"Yeah. Tina Esparza."

Meg cleared her throat noisily.

"And, uh, this is my friend Meg Janis."

Dave grinned. "Hi, Meg."

"Nice to meet you, Dave," Meg said, smiling even more. "And thanks for the tips on heading the ball. I can never do that right. Maybe you can help me sometime."

Oh, good grief! Tina thought. When it came to boys, Meg was unbelievable.

"I play soccer too," said Dave. "I'm looking for a team to play with. Is it okay if I kick the ball around a little with you?"

Meg spoke first, while Tina was getting the ball out of the bushes. "Sure!" she said. "It's always better with three people than with two. There are lots of teams around. You won't have any trouble getting on one of them. Do you play any position in particular?"

Tina chipped the ball to Dave, who headed it perfectly to Meg. He said, "I was a defenseman last year, but I could be a wing too. I'm pretty fast. I'll play any position, just so I can be on a team."

Staring at Dave, Meg let the ball go past her. Tina giggled, and Meg glared at her.

As they played, Tina decided that Dave *was* a pretty good player and that Meg didn't care how good he was, as long as he had those blue eyes and that blond hair.

"Uh-oh," Dave said, looking at his watch. "This is fun, but I'd better go home. I have stuff to do before dinner. Nice meeting you, Meg. I guess I'll see you both at school."

"See you," replied Tina.

"We'll *definitely* see you!" Meg said, with another of her big, dumb smiles.

After Dave had gone inside, Tina snickered. "We'll *definitely* see you!" she mimicked, putting a sappy grin on her face.

"What's wrong with what I said?" Meg demanded. "Is he or is he not a nice boy?"

Tina shrugged. "I guess, yeah."

"Is it a crime to be nice to a nice boy?"

Tina kicked the ball into the open garage door. "No, it's not," she admitted.

Meg sat on the grass. "Well, okay. You might think about being nice to him, too."

Tina sat down facing her friend. "Me? I *was* nice! I didn't say anything mean, did I?"

"No, you didn't say anything mean. You hardly said anything at all!" Meg said. "Why?"

"I don't know," Tina said. "I didn't have anything to say. I didn't know *what* to say."

Meg waved her hands in frustration. "You could have talked about soccer or if he likes his teachers. You could've talked about his favorite music or *your* favorite music or if pizza is better with mushrooms or sausages. You could've talked about anything!"

Tina stared at the grass. "When you say it, it sounds so easy. When you talk to people, you act like you're enjoying it."

"I *am* enjoying it! And it *is* easy!"

"For you!" Tina snapped. "Not me! I open my mouth and try to think of what to say and nothing comes out. So I feel stupid, which means that more nothing comes out! And don't ask why, because I don't know!"

There was a silence, which Meg broke. "I'm sorry. I know it's hard for you. And I wish I had some ideas to help, but I don't.

"Except, now you have this cute next-door neighbor. Can you *talk* to him a little? It'd be good practice. And he's going to make new friends, who could become *your* friends, and you could talk to them too. It would be a start."

Tina stood up. "You're right. I'll try. I know I should do it, so I'll talk to him. It's just . . . it's not going to be easy, that's all."

Meg stood up too. "Maybe it won't be as hard as you think." She laughed. "I can tell you one thing — if Dave was *my* neighbor, I sure wouldn't have any trouble at all!"

In spite of herself, Tina couldn't help laughing too. Meg was just Meg, especially when it came to boys.

2

Are you coming straight home from school today?"
Mrs. Esparza asked Tina.

"No, Mom," Tina said. "I have soccer practice, remember?"

The Esparza family was having breakfast. Next to Tina, her eight-year-old brother, Sammy, made a face as he played with his cereal. "Soccer is lame. Baseball rules!"

"Hey!" said Mr. Esparza. "Don't knock soccer. It's the world's most popular sport. *And* it's the most popular sport in this house, two to one. Right, sweetie?"

"Right, Dad," Tina replied.

"Mom loves baseball," Sammy said. "So it's a tie for most popular sport in the house."

Mrs. Esparza smiled. "Sammy, you know I'll cheer for you in baseball games, and I'll cheer for Tina in soccer games. But I don't have a favorite sport. To me, they're both the same — impossible to understand."

Mr. Esparza sighed. "Now that, *I* don't understand. Baseball, sure, that's hard to follow. But soccer is as natural as breathing. Is breathing hard to understand?"

Mr. Esparza had grown up in Argentina and played soccer — or *futbol,* as he sometimes called it — throughout his early years. He'd injured his knee as a young man and had to stop playing. But he followed the sport, rooting for Argentina in big international events such as the World Cup. When his old "home team," the Boca Juniors, was on cable TV, he watched.

Mr. Esparza loved to talk about the great Argentine soccer stars he had seen, such as Maradona and DiStefano. Finally, even Tina, who loved soccer, would roll her eyes.

"Daddy," she'd say. "I've heard this all before. Like, maybe a hundred times."

"I'm never tired of talking about those great athletes," her father would reply. "But, okay. I'll stop for now."

Today, however, Tina was lucky. He didn't start off on the old-timers. He only said, "How do you feel about this new team?"

Tina took a last swallow of milk. "Okay, I guess. Well, a little nervous."

"Nervous?" he repeated. "Why? You'll do fine! You're very good! I ought to know, I've seen some of the greatest —"

"Yes, Daddy," she interrupted. "Maradona, and all those guys. But this team is better than the ones I've played with. Maybe I'm not good enough yet. Some of these girls will be two years older than me, and more experienced."

Mr. Esparza waved these worries off. "You'll be fine. You're very good for your age. Plus, soccer is in your blood. You wait and see, you'll be a star."

That wasn't what Tina wanted to hear, though her father had no way of knowing it. Mrs. Esparza must have seen something in her daughter's face, though, because she said, "Even if you're not a star, honey, you'll have fun. And I'm sure you'll be good enough for the team."

"Sure you will!" Sammy said. "I'll go to your games and hold up signs and everything."

13

Tina joined the laughter at Sammy's enthusiasm, but she was definitely nervous; she was trembling inside. It was partly because she was worried about whether she would be good enough, but it was also because she knew that a new team meant a new coach and teammates. *Strangers.* She couldn't bring herself to talk about these fears. Her family wouldn't get it.

Tina lived a few blocks from school, and on nice days, she liked to walk. As she headed down the front path, shrugging into her backpack, Dave came out of his yard and smiled at her.

"Hi! Mind if I walk with you?"

Tina couldn't see any nice way of turning him down, and Meg's advice about being nice was in her mind, so she smiled and said, "I don't mind. Let's go."

Before she could work herself into a panic about what to say, Dave solved the problem by speaking first.

"I hate starting in a new school. Being the new kid. You don't know anyone, you don't know where people hang out. It's the worst."

Tina nodded. "It must be pretty bad. I don't know what I'd do if it were me. I'm not good with people I don't know."

"Me neither," Dave said. "I always feel like I'm taking some kind of test that I'll probably fail. They'll think, 'What a wuss.'"

Tina was surprised to hear somebody else say things that she might say. She always figured that her problems were special and that few others shared them. But here was this boy, a boy that Meg thought was cute, who said that he had trouble dealing with new faces. Amazing! She found herself in the un-usual position of wanting to make him feel better.

"Well, *I* don't think you're a wuss," she said. "Nei-ther does my friend Meg. And I bet no one else will, either."

Dave smiled gratefully. "Thanks. It's good to hear you say that. Because, sometimes, you know, I'm not too sure what . . . well, what other people think about me. Especially girls."

Tina smiled. "I have the same problem. I mean, I'm not really great with other people, either. Espe-cially a big group of them together."

Dave turned and stared at her. "Really? Huh." He thought for a moment, then said, "It's funny. I just figure it's a problem I have that most people don't."

Tina adjusted her backpack. "I always think it's just *me*. I mean, I have my first soccer practice this afternoon, and I'm really nervous. Not just because I may not be good enough, but because there'll be a coach and players I don't know. That's even worse."

Tina was finding it easier to talk to Dave than she had expected, even about subjects she usually kept to herself. They were at school before she knew it.

"Good luck at soccer today," said Dave as they went inside. "I bet you'll do great."

"Thanks," Tina answered. "And I bet you'll make lots of new friends really soon."

Dave grinned. "I've made one or two already."

The school day passed without a problem. After school, Tina walked home, then she biked to Meg's house. The girls rode to the field where the Wildcats were to meet for practice. They brought their soccer shoes — with aluminum studs on the bottoms so that they wouldn't slip on wet grass or mud — and shin guards. Tina mentioned walking to school with Dave.

"He was nice," Tina said. "Speaking of nice, I hope this new coach is nice. I —"

"Did he talk about me?" Meg demanded.

Tina was a little annoyed by Meg's one-track mind. "I didn't . . . well, he said that he was glad to have made two friends here. I guess he meant you and me."

Meg said, "I was hoping we'd have some of the same classes, but I didn't see him. But maybe we'll see him at lunch sometime."

Before Tina could turn the conversation back to soccer, they had arrived at the field.

Among the girls already there, talking, lacing up their shoes, and stretching, were some Tina was happy to recognize: teammates from past years and a few she knew a little at school.

Two women were setting up bright-orange traffic cones on the field. One of them had to be Danielle. A couple of girls waved and called hello to Tina and Meg. Tina laced her shoes, telling herself to relax, that there was nothing to be nervous about.

As Tina finished tucking her molded plastic shin guards in place under her knee-length socks, she heard a shrill whistle. One of the women signaled for the girls to gather around her. She was tall, with curly brown hair held in place by a red sweatband. She wore a yellow workout suit and held a clipboard.

She smiled brightly. "It's good to see so many of you. It looks like we have eighteen players here — that's excellent.

"My name is Danielle Barron. I've been a coach for several years, and I played soccer in college and, for a time, professionally as well."

Danielle gestured to the woman standing at her side. She was not as tall as Danielle, had short, glossy black hair, and wore shorts and a sweatshirt. "This is Pepper Schmidt, my assistant. She was a top college player and really knows the game. For part of our practices, we'll split the team in half, and Pepper and I will each work with a group. Before anything else, I'd like each of you to call out your name so that we get to know each other."

When her turn came, Tina shouted out as well as everyone else, which was a relief to her.

After the introductions, Danielle said, "I believe we can have a successful season, and here's what I mean by success." She ticked off the points on her fingers. "You all have a good time; you all give your best effort; you all get to play meaningful minutes;

you all play *as a team.* If we do that, we'll have a great year.

"Playing as a team means that when you're in the game you know where the ball is, what the situation is, and what your job is. A team that plays as a unit will almost always beat a team with one or two out-standing players trying to do it on their own. Soccer is the ultimate *team* sport. Anyway, that's how I coach. I hope you have shin guards, because you can't play without them. Any questions?"

There were no questions. Tina liked what Danielle had said. It fit in with her goal of not standing out. As she glanced around, she noticed that a few girls looked doubtful. Maybe they didn't like the fact that Danielle didn't see winning as the only thing that mattered. Maybe they saw themselves as stars and didn't like Danielle's downplaying of the role of stars. But maybe Tina was misreading the expressions on the girls' faces, and they were as happy with the coach as she was.

Danielle divided the team in half and took her half to the far end of the field to work. Pepper stayed with the others, including Tina and Meg. Pepper gathered them together behind a line of orange traffic cones that were five feet apart. She rolled a soccer ball in front of one of the girls.

"We're going to do a dribbling exercise. I want each of you to dribble the ball, weaving around those cones; go to the left of the first cone, to the right of the second one, and so on, to the end of the line. Then come back, doing the same thing. Remember, use only your feet. Okay? *Go!*"

Tina watched the first girl, who did well until she mis-hit the ball so it rolled away. She looked at Pepper, not sure what to do.

"It's okay," Pepper said. "Just get the ball and finish the course."

On Meg's turn, she went through the cones carefully, not losing the ball, but taking more time than the other players. Pepper said nothing. Tina got through faster because she used the outside as well as the inside edges of her feet to move the ball along.

After they finished, Pepper said, "Good! Here are things to work on. First, you should dribble without watching your feet. In a game, you need to keep your eyes on the field and other players, or a defender might steal the ball before you know what's happening. Or you might miss a chance for a pass to set up an attack or a shot. Practice until it feels natural to look up as you dribble.

"Another thing: Did you see how Tina — is that your name?"

Tina blushed and nodded wordlessly.

"— how Tina was faster through the cones because she used both the inside *and* outside edges of her feet? Practice that too. Let's do it one more time."

The girls went through again. Some were better, but a few, trying not to look down, lost control of the ball.

"Don't worry," Pepper said. "You'll improve with practice. Before long, it'll be natural. Let's work on passing."

Pepper paired off the girls and had each pair place two cones five feet apart. The players stood thirty feet from each other with the cones midway between them. The coach gave each twosome a ball and partnered herself with Meg.

"What you do," she said, "is pass to each other, between the cones." She demonstrated, kicking the ball to Meg. "See how I kick with the inner surface of my foot? You can't control the ball when you kick with your toes. Okay?"

Tina already knew the technique and did fine, as did other girls with a lot of soccer experience. A few had trouble getting the ball between the cones. Pepper knelt by one of the girls. "First, *plant* the foot you're not kicking with, and then *swing* your other leg so the inside surface of the foot hits the ball. Lock the ankle of your kicking foot — don't flex it."

The girl's next pass was between the cones. The players worked on passing with both right and left feet. After a while, Pepper moved them ten feet farther apart.

"Great!" Pepper said, after the drill was over. "You're all getting the idea. Now for some passing on the run."

She had pairs of players run twenty yards one way and back the other way, passing to each other as they ran. Tina quickly realized that her partner didn't know how to pass on the move. Her partner's first pass was yards behind her, forcing Tina to stop short and backpedal. The other girl then lofted her next kick high in the air, forcing Tina to lunge forward and stop the ball with her forehead. So it went, up and down the field. Tina was embarrassed for the other girl and herself. At one point, the other girl, whom

Tina didn't know, actually gave Tina an annoyed look, as if everything was Tina's fault. Tina, who had just made a desperate but unsuccessful try to reach another bad pass, said nothing. She did notice, however, that Pepper was watching them closely.

Afterward, Pepper said, "Remember: When you pass, lock the ankle — don't flex it. Swing your foot in a line toward the receiver and allow for her being a moving target." She didn't say a word to Tina's partner, but Tina realized that Pepper knew what had happened.

Pepper then split the group into threes. Two players would pass back and forth, with the third as a defender trying to intercept passes.

Tina was relieved when the girl who couldn't pass well was put in a different group. Tina's threesome included Meg and a third girl, who could pass. Tina and the other girl, a tall redhead named Zoe, had little trouble keeping the ball away from Meg. Meg was slow to react and see where the ball was going.

Then Tina was the defender. On Meg's first pass, Meg almost came to a full stop and looked hard at Zoe before kicking. Tina easily intercepted. Zoe managed to get the ball by Tina, but Tina picked off

Meg's second pass too. She could have intercepted almost every pass Meg made because Meg did everything but yell, "I'm going to pass now" before passing. But Tina felt bad for Meg and deliberately let passes through. She thought that Pepper knew what she was doing. She did it anyway.

After the drill, Pepper said, "Be careful not to let defenders know you're going to pass or who you're passing to. Kick on the run, and don't stare at your target. Tina, good 'D'!"

Once again, Tina felt uncomfortable at being singled out, even for praise. A minute later, Pepper came up to Tina and said softly, so no one else heard, "Meg's a good friend, right?"

Tina turned red and nodded.

"I understand," Pepper said. "But try not to be embarrassed about being a good athlete."

Again Tina nodded but said nothing.

Pepper studied Tina for a moment, smiled at her, and went to pick up the cones.

The team took a break. Danielle and Pepper huddled together, and at one point, Tina thought she caught them looking her way.

Meg came up to Tina while the coaches talked.

24

"You were taking it easy on me in that last drill. You don't have to. I know you're better at this than I am, and I'm okay with it."

"Pepper sort of told me the same thing just now," Tina admitted.

"She's right," said Meg.

After the break, Danielle took over Tina's group. She set up a shooting drill in which two players tried to set up shots while a third girl acted as goalkeeper. Danielle used cones to mark off a goal.

Tina passed to Zoe, who slammed a hard shot past the girl in goal. A few minutes later, Tina aimed a shot at the corner of the goal, but it was just wide.

Then it was Tina's turn to act as keeper.

On the first shot — kicked by Zoe — Tina dived to one side and stretched out to catch the ball. Out of the corner of her eye, Tina saw Danielle give an approving nod. A few minutes later, Zoe and a girl Tina didn't know moved in, passing back and forth until they were five yards away. Tina moved toward the girl with the ball, who tried to kick it past her. Tina just got a hand on it and knocked it away. She stopped all but one shot attempt during her turn as goalkeeper.

On the last shot, Zoe tried to chip the ball over Tina's head. Tina leaped up as high as she could, punched the ball straight up, and stepped back to grab the ball as it came down.

"Good save!" Danielle called.

Tina smiled weakly, knowing that her face was bright red.

Practice ended soon after the goalkeeping drill. As Tina was getting ready to leave, Danielle called to her.

Tina felt nervous for no clear reason, but walked over to the coach.

"Have you ever been a goalkeeper?" the coach asked.

Tina shook her head. "No. I've usually been a mid-fielder."

"Interesting," Danielle said. "You have good goal-keeping instincts. Instead of backing away from a shooter, you knew when to go *toward* her and cut down her target. You're also fast when you move to either side."

"Uh . . . thanks," Tina mumbled. She didn't like where this conversation was going.

"Are you interested in goalkeeping?" the coach

asked. "It's an important position, and our top keeper from last year is gone."

Tina didn't want to simply say no, even though that was how she felt. Finally, she said, "Well . . . I don't know."

"It's all right," said Danielle. "I don't need a definite answer right now, but I'd like you to think about it, okay? If you decide you'd rather not, fine. You'll be a good addition to the Wildcats in any position."

"Thanks," said Tina. Walking away, she was worried. The more she thought about goalkeeping, the less she liked it. It was the one position where you couldn't be invisible. Keepers even wore different-colored uniforms, so players could distinguish them from their teammates. Playing keeper carried more responsibility.

On the other hand, Danielle said that the Wildcats needed a good keeper. The thought that she might be letting the team down was troubling to Tina. She didn't know what to do. Why did things have to get so complicated?

3

What did Danielle want?" asked Meg as the girls headed home. "You look like you just got bad news."

Tina sighed. "She thinks I should be a goalkeeper."

"Really?" Meg said. "That's great! Isn't it? You'll be awesome! I wish I was as quick as you. I'd love to be a keeper."

"Well, not me," said Tina. "Goalkeepers are always in the spotlight. If they make saves, they're heroes, and if the other team scores, they're booed. I'd hate it either way."

"But it isn't just the keeper's fault when the other team scores," objected Meg.

"No, but a lot of people think it is. I don't want to stand out. I just want to fit in."

"I know how you feel," said Meg. "Except the thing is, Danielle's right. You'd be so good! We'd be a better team with you there. Will you think about it?"

"Yeah, I'll think about it," Tina said, looking unhappy.

"Here's something else to think about," Meg added. "If you're an awesome goalkeeper, like I think you'll be, it'll be good for you."

"Yeah?" Tina replied. "How?"

"You have trouble with people paying a lot of attention to you. But if you become an important player on the Wildcats, people are *going* to pay more attention to you."

Tina stared at her friend. "How will that be good for me?"

Meg said, "Think about it, Teen! You don't like being in the spotlight, because you're not used to it. But the more you're *in* the spotlight, the more you'll get used to it! As you get used to it, you'll have an easier time with it. Wait and see."

Tina thought about what Meg had said as they reached Tina's house.

"You really think so?" she asked.

But Meg didn't answer. She was looking toward Dave's house.

"Is Dave around?" Meg asked.

"How should I know?" Tina snapped, annoyed. "I thought we were talking, but if you'd rather look for *Dave*, see if I care!"

Meg blinked. "I was only —"

Tina cut her off. "You were only! If you'd rather see *Dave*, go knock on his door. I thought you wanted to spend time with me, but maybe I was wrong."

"I'm sorry, Teen." Meg looked like she meant it. "You're my best friend, and I didn't mean I wanted to see Dave and not you. But you know me. I like spending time with boys. Dave happens to be a nice boy — even you say so — and I was wondering if he was home. I didn't mean to hurt your feelings."

Tina knew right away that she had overreacted. "It's okay. I'm too touchy."

Meg said, "Let's just forget it." She sat on the grass. "I was wondering something. Do you feel more shy with boys than with girls?"

Tina thought for a moment. "I don't think so. I feel that way with anyone I don't know well, whether it's a boy or a girl. But I don't know as many boys."

"Do you have any idea why you have trouble just

relaxing around other kids?" asked Meg. Then she hastily added, "If you'd rather not talk about it . . ."

"No, it's all right," Tina assured her. She sat down next to her friend. "I think about it sometimes. I guess I'm afraid I'm really boring, that nothing I have to say could interest anyone. When I'm with other people, I try to think of stuff to say and I can't and . . . well, then I *am* boring. Either I don't say anything or I say dumb things, until people want to get away from me before they start yawning in my face. Or snoring."

"Huh," said Meg. "That's weird. You're not like that at all when it's just you and me, and no one else is around. You have plenty to say, and you can be funny too. Too bad other kids never see that side of you."

Tina smiled. Meg was a good friend and wanted Tina to feel better about herself, but Tina didn't believe a word of it.

Just then, Dave came out of his house and saw the girls. "Hey! Hi!"

Meg's face lit up, and Tina smiled as convincingly as she could.

"What's happening?" Dave asked.

"Not much," said Tina.

"We just had our first soccer practice," Meg said.

"Yeah?" Dave leaned against the Esparzas' fence. "How was it? How's the coach? Tina, you said you were nervous about her."

"She's nice," Meg said. "And she thinks Tina could be a star goalkeeper."

"No kidding!" Dave grinned at Tina. "Fantastic! That'd be great!"

Tina shrugged, looking down at the grass. "I don't know. Meg is exaggerating. And I don't know if I want to."

"Why not?" Dave asked. "I think it'd be fantastic to be a good keeper. But I don't have the talent. I guess you do."

"Tina's a super athlete," Meg said. "She doesn't think so, but she is. How's school? You like your teachers?"

"Yeah, they're okay," Dave said. "I really like my science teacher, Mr. Ryan. He's cool. You know him?"

Tina nodded but said nothing. Meg asked, "Is Mr. Ryan the tall guy with the mustache? He seems nice."

"Yeah, that's him. Tina, don't you take science?"

32

Dave squatted on the edge of the lawn. "It's my favorite subject. What's yours?"

Tina shrugged. "I don't know. They're all okay, I guess."

"*My* favorite is English," Meg said. "I love reading. Tina's really good in English too. She's an awesome writer."

"Really?" Dave asked. "I wish I wrote well, but I'm not good at it. Maybe you could help me, I mean, if you have the time."

There was a long, awkward silence. Meg turned and stared hard at Tina. "I bet Tina *could* help, right, Tina?"

Very softly, Tina said, "Maybe. I guess. I'm not really that good."

"Oh," Dave said. Meg cleared her throat and was about to speak when Dave suddenly stood up. "See you," he said, walked back to his house, and went inside.

Tina looked up, surprised. "Why did he jump up and go like that?" she asked.

Meg laughed. "You're kidding, right?"

"No, I'm not," Tina said. "What happened?"

Meg shook her head and spoke slowly to Tina, as

33

if she was talking to someone who was not too bright. "What happened is that Dave saw that you weren't interested in him, and he felt bad, so he left. That's what happened."

"That's just silly!" Tina was puzzled by what Meg said, "Why should he care if I'm interested in him or not?"

Meg wore an expression of comic disbelief. "Tee-*NUH!* Come *on!* Are you really, truly telling me you didn't know that Dave likes you?"

Tina was stunned. "*Likes* me? What do you mean?"

Meg shook her head. "Oh, boy. Teen, listen. Dave likes you. Couldn't you tell? The whole time he was here, he was staring at you. I was hoping he'd be interested in me, but no way. He talked to *you*. He asked *you* if you took science. He asked what *your* favorite subject was. He asked *you* to help him with English. You, you, you. You paid no attention to him at *all*. So he got the picture and left."

Tina was amazed. Could Meg possibly be right? "But I wasn't nasty to him, was I? I don't think I was, anyway."

Meg shook her head. "You weren't nasty. You

weren't *anything.* You just wouldn't talk to him or even look at him. He got the hint."

"*What* hint?" Tina demanded, still bewildered. "I wasn't giving him any hint."

Meg looked a little sad. "I guess you weren't. But when a boy has a crush on you, and you don't talk to him, well . . ."

"A *crush!* Oh, stop it! That's just silly!"

"It's the truth," Meg said calmly.

Tina was uncomfortable. "This is . . . I don't want to talk about that anymore, okay?"

"Sure," Meg said. "But I'm right. I *know* I am. But we can talk about something else."

"Good!" Tina said.

"What do you want to talk about?" asked Meg.

Tina said, "I don't know. Nothing, I guess."

Meg sighed and said, "Well, I should go home anyway. You're not mad at me, are you?"

"No, why should I be?" Tina felt confused and wanted to be alone. "I still don't think you're right, though."

"Well, let's not talk about Dave anymore. Except, it would still be good practice to be nice to him, and he *is* nice. But forget it. I'll see you tomorrow."

Tina waved to Meg as Meg got on her bike. Then she lay back in the grass and stared at the sky, thinking. What should she tell Danielle? Would she try being a goalkeeper? Could she handle it?

Was Meg right about Dave liking her?

And how did *she* feel about *Dave?*

4

On Saturday morning, the Esparzas had a late breakfast. Tina had soccer practice later but had nothing to do until Meg came by to get her. Mr. Esparza poured himself a cup of coffee.

"How's the new team and new coach?"

"Pretty good," Tina said. "I like the coach, Danielle. She's nice. Except . . ."

"Except what?" her father asked.

"She wants me to try being a keeper."

Mr. Esparza smiled. "Yes? Terrific!"

"I don't know," Tina said.

Her father said, "No? It's an important position. It's great that your coach wants you to play it. The goalkeeper can be the heart of a team. I know you can be very good at it."

Tina said, "Well, I — you do?"

"Absolutely. I've been watching you play for years, and I know how good you are, how strong, what kind of athlete you are."

"But I've never been a star or anything."

"It doesn't matter," he replied. "You have what it takes. And don't think I'm just being a proud papa. If I didn't think you had the talent, I wouldn't say it. But you do."

Mrs. Esparza patted her daughter's hand. "Your father would never say what he didn't believe. What he tells you, he means."

"Daddy's right," said Sammy.

Mr. Esparza's face grew serious. "I know you're not sure about goalkeeping, but I hope you try it before you make up your mind. Your coach is sharp if she can already see how good you are. I see you're not as sure of yourself as your mother and I are of you."

"And me too," Sammy said.

"But, you know?" Mr. Esparza went on. "I'd rather have a daughter who's a little unsure of herself than one who's *too* sure of herself. You'll do the right thing, I know."

Tina was touched. "Thanks, Daddy," she said. "And I *will* give it a try."

Mr. Esparza nodded. "Good. See what you have in you. That's all I want."

There was a knock at the door. "Teen? You there?" It was Meg.

"Come in!" Tina called. "We're finishing breakfast."

Meg came in with her canvas sports bag. "Hi, Mr. Esparza, Mrs. Esparza. Hey, Sammy, what's happening?"

"Yo, Meg, what's happening?" called Sammy, standing and raising his hand for a high-five. Meg slapped his hand with hers.

"How are you doing?" Tina asked.

"Okay," said Meg. "Did you decide what to do about goalkeeping yet?"

"I'm going to try it," Tina replied. "Unless Danielle changes her mind, which would be all right too."

"Good deal!" Meg said happily. "You're going to be great, I just know it!"

"That's what I said," said Mr. Esparza.

"Me too!" yelled Sammy.

The girls rode to the practice field, and while Meg put on her soccer shoes and shin guards, Tina found Danielle and Pepper.

"About being a keeper," Tina said. "Okay. I'll try it. If you still want me to, I mean. If you changed your mind . . ."

"No, I haven't," Danielle said. "That's good news."

"Okay," Tina said, nervous about what she had committed herself to. "So, what now?"

"You'll mostly do what everyone else does," said Danielle. "Dribbling, passing, shooting, defense. I want every player to have some understanding of every position, every part of the sport. But you'll also work on goalkeeping with me or with Pepper. And we'll train at least one other player — so we have a keeper ready, in case you're out of action."

Tina said, "Okay, then. Thanks."

"I think you have the potential to be a good goal-keeper," Pepper said. "You already have a sense of what it's about."

Tina felt better about her choice after talking to the coaches. They'd been encouraging.

Practice began like the last one, with work on the same skills. This time, Tina was in Danielle's group, but Meg wasn't. For dribbling, Danielle did what she called "follow the leader." The groups split into pairs. The leader of each pair, who had no ball, ran around the field, turning left and right in no particular pattern. The other girl in each pair had to follow the leader while dribbling a ball. Because the dribbler had to watch the leader and other players on the field, she couldn't look at her feet. After a while, the leaders and followers switched places.

Tina was able to stay with her leader, Zoe, though a couple of girls nearly ran into her because they had to look down now and then so as not to lose the ball. Later, Danielle advised everyone to keep working on dribbling.

For passing, Danielle divided players into groups of three. Each group formed a line, with the end girls ten yards apart and the middle girl midway between them. Each end player had a ball. One would pass to the middle player, who controlled the ball and passed it back. The middle player then turned to take a pass from the other end and pass *that* ball back. The middle player had to pivot and pass quickly and accurately. Players switched so that everyone got to play in the middle. Tina found that being in the middle made her speed up more than she was used to, pivoting and getting her passes off in less time. It was a challenge, she thought.

Danielle gave some tips on controlling low passes by stopping the ball under one foot, and on controlling high passes by taking the ball on the chest or thigh and letting it drop.

Next was a shooting drill. Danielle used cones to mark off a regulation goal — eight yards wide — and had pairs of players attack it, passing the ball three times before taking a shot. Then she put a player in as a goalkeeper to defend against shots. Finally, the coach used more cones to create one-yard-wide targets at each end of the goal and had players shoot for either side from fifteen feet away.

Tina was not an accurate shooter, missing two of four shots at the narrow openings. The best in the group was Zoe, who hit all her attempts. Another girl, whom Tina didn't know, was also very good. After this girl booted in a sizzling score that went across the goalmouth — a tough angle — Tina said, "Nice shot."

The other girl nodded without smiling or even looking at Tina. Zoe and Tina exchanged looks, and Zoe rolled her eyes, making Tina grin even though she felt hurt.

When Danielle called for a break, Tina whispered to Zoe, "Who is that girl?"

"Cindy Vane," replied Zoe. "Don't worry, she's like that with lots of people."

Tina felt a little better, but not much. Meg came over. "How was your practice? Ours was pretty good. I like Pepper."

"I think they're both good," Tina said.

"Did you do any goalkeeping work?"

Tina shook her head. "Not yet."

"Tina?" Pepper appeared behind Tina's shoulder. "Ready for some goalkeeper drills? I'd like to start today."

Tina felt a tingle of nervousness, which she fought not to show. "Sure, whenever."

Pepper smiled. "Good. As soon as we get back to work, I'll take you and another girl who's also going to work on being a keeper, and we can get going."

As Pepper walked over to talk to Danielle, Tina looked at Meg, not bothering to hide her nervousness.

"You'll be great!" said Meg. "You'll see. You're going to be a great keeper."

"Definitely," Zoe agreed. "I can tell you're a really good athlete."

Tina, who had trouble replying to compliments, shrugged and mumbled, "Thanks, but I don't know . . ."

"Hey, do you two want to come to the mall with me after practice?" Zoe asked. "Some of my friends hang out there on Saturdays. It's fun."

"I don't know if I can," Tina said, looking at Meg and hoping she would turn the invitation down.

But Meg said, "Sounds good. I tell you what, let's see after we're done, all right?"

Tina felt as if she'd been pushed into a corner, but said only, "Okay, we'll see."

Danielle blew her whistle, the signal to start practice again. Meg leaned in toward Tina. "Come on, Teen! Why not go? It might be fun!"

Tina knew that hanging out at the mall with girls she didn't know wouldn't be fun. But she also knew that Meg wanted to go, and she didn't want to disappoint her friend.

"Let me think it over, okay?" she said.

"Teen, this is the kind of thing you need to do,"

Meg said. "To try to be more friendly with people. We talked about it before, and here's a chance to really do it."

Tina saw the truth of this but didn't feel any more eager to go to the mall. "We'll see," she said, and ran to join Pepper before Meg could say anything else.

Standing with Pepper was a girl Tina recognized from school. She was taller than Tina, and her dark-blond hair was short and curly. She smiled at Tina, who smiled back.

"You know each other?" Pepper asked.

"I think I've met you," said the other girl. "Tina, right?"

Tina nodded. "Right. I'm Tina Esparza. And your name is . . . Andrea?"

"Uh-huh, Andrea Gries. I've never been a goal-keeper. I guess I could be your backup."

Tina shook her head. "I was never a keeper, either. Maybe I'll be *your* backup."

Tina thought Andrea seemed nice. Andrea was taller, so it would probably be easier for her to reach high shots. Well, even if Andrea was a better keeper, Tina would do her best and that would be that.

Pepper demonstrated a standard keeper's stance: feet shoulders' width apart, knees slightly bent, body leaning slightly forward.

"Bend your arms with your forearms forward and your hands alongside your legs," Pepper said, as the girls followed her instructions. "Spread your fingers and turn your hands so your palms face toward where a ball would be coming. Good!"

From this position, Tina saw that she'd be able to react quickly in any direction.

"Now we'll work on catching balls when shots are made," said Pepper. "First, here's what we call the W-catch, which you use to take a high shot. Tina, throw me the ball so it's at my eye level."

Pepper caught Tina's throw with her fingers outspread and her thumbs together. She turned to Tina and Andrea. "See how my thumbs and index fingers form a letter W on the ball? Let's see you try it."

Pepper went on to techniques for catching lower shots: the scoop catch for ground-level shots and the chest catch for medium-high shots. She threw the ball to Andrea so Andrea could try a chest catch.

"Good, Andrea. Bring the ball in toward your body with your arms around it so you won't drop it and give an opponent an easy shot. Same with the scoop catch: bend your knees deep, palms toward the ball, and cradle it so you won't drop it. Then, straighten up and decide what to do with it."

"What *do* I do with it?" asked Andrea, after she'd done a scoop catch.

"It depends," answered Pepper. "That's something for another day. For now, we'll stick to basic moves."

Pepper handed balls to the girls and told them to bounce them like basketballs. She stopped them after a moment.

"Don't use your palms, use your fingers. You control the ball better that way. Practice on your own. Here's another exercise to do on your own."

Pepper had the girls lie on their backs and throw balls in the air, away from their bodies. They then jumped to their feet and tried to catch the balls before they hit the ground.

"Dive for the ball if you have to," Pepper said. "This exercise will speed up your reactions and movement."

The first time Tina tossed a ball up, it hit the ground before she could reach it. The second time, she leaped up and lunged forward to catch the ball at shoe-top height. She tried a few more times and thought she was improving.

"Good!" called Pepper.

Andrea had trouble getting her feet under her and was unable to catch the ball.

"It's okay," said Pepper. "You'll get better."

The coach then had the girls do drills together. First, they threw a ball back and forth, sometimes high and sometimes low, to work on catching. Then they faced each other, six feet apart, and took turns rolling a ball toward each other. The receiver would stoop, kneel, or dive to control the ball. Andrea's long fingers made it a little easier for her than it was for Tina.

Tina was surprised when Pepper said that it was time to join the rest of the team. She'd been enjoying the drills and didn't realize how much time had passed.

Practice finished with some three-on-three scrimmages, with both coaches watching and occasionally calling out suggestions. Tina realized that her favorite part of the whole session had been the goalkeeping work.

When practice ended for the day, Danielle beckoned to Tina. "Pepper says that you did well in the goalkeeping workout. Are you feeling more confident about being a keeper?"

Tina decided to simply tell the coach the truth. "Not really," she said. "But I'm still willing to work on it. I just don't know if I want to do it, I mean in games."

"Okay," replied Danielle. "Just remember — I'll never push you to do anything you'd rather not do. But I'd like to know why you're uncomfortable with being a goalkeeper."

Feeling very self-conscious, Tina didn't say anything for a moment. Finally, she blurted, "This is going to sound really dumb."

Danielle smiled. "I promise you, I'm only asking out of curiosity. And it's strictly between the two of us."

"Okay," said Tina. "It's . . . I hate being the center of attention. And a keeper is going to be the center of attention a lot, whether she does great or she messes up. It's not that I'm afraid of the responsibility. You see?"

To Tina's surprise, Danielle said, "Sure. You're not the first girl I've worked with who's felt that way. There have been others. Sometimes they over-came the feeling and sometimes not. The ones that didn't — they went back to playing positions where they felt relaxed. If you decide goalkeeping isn't for you, we'll end the experiment. But until you're sure, I'd like you to stay with it. Okay?"

This seemed fair to Tina. "Fine."

Danielle grinned. "All right. See you."

Smiling, Tina looked for Meg. She saw Meg with Zoe, and her smile vanished.

It looked like she was going to have to go to the mall and "hang out." With a bunch of strangers.

5

As Tina slowly walked toward Meg and Zoe, she noticed two things. She saw Cindy and a few other players watching her. Tina was sure they were talking about her — probably about how weird she was.

She also noticed that Meg and Zoe were trying very hard to look like they had *not* been talking about her, which, of course, meant that they *had* been. Meg had probably told Zoe that Tina was kind of, you know, shy, and would be unhappy about going to the mall, and that Zoe should really try to see that Tina was included in the group so Tina would feel more at ease.

All this made Tina feel the exact opposite of "at ease." But she had made up her mind. Tina would do what Meg wanted because *(a)* Meg was her best friend and wanted Tina to go, and *(b)* Meg felt it would be good for Tina, and she might even be right.

"Hi," she said to Meg and Zoe.

"So, what do you think?" asked Meg, glancing quickly at Zoe. "You want to go?"

Tina couldn't fake enthusiasm for going, but she managed to nod and say, "Sure."

"Great!" said Zoe, and the girls got their bikes.

"We don't have to stick around all day," Meg said to Tina as they rode. "And maybe you'll even like it."

"Sure, maybe I will," Tina replied, managing a smile. Then she hung back, leaving Meg to chat happily with Zoe. Meg was obviously looking forward to this.

It wasn't that Tina hated malls or never went to the one nearby. She went, now and then. She sometimes shopped for clothes there with her mom, and sometimes she and Meg went to the movies. But Tina never hung out with other kids at the mall or anywhere else.

Tina knew how it would be. She'd sit there trying to think of stuff to say, and nothing would come out of her mouth. Everyone else would talk and laugh and have a great time, and Tina would sit like a lump. Other girls would wonder what *her* problem was, and it would only get worse, until finally it would be time to go home.

They locked up their bikes in the mall parking area, and Zoe led them toward the Food Court, where a dozen fast-food places sold all kinds of stuff and there was a big central area full of tables and chairs. Sure enough, a group of a dozen girls sat together, chatting and giggling. Tina felt herself getting stiff and uncomfortable. A couple of the girls looked up, spotted Zoe, and waved. Zoe waved back and started in their direction, with Meg following eagerly and Tina bringing up the rear.

Zoe introduced Tina and Meg to everyone. Tina heard a bunch of names: Cilla, Jane, Maddy, Lynn, Annette, Tiffany . . . she couldn't remember which girl went with which name. She had met or at least seen a few of the girls at school, but she wasn't even sure which ones. Tina sat down on the edge of the group and smiled and waited for it to be over.

Zoe sat down next to her. "How do you like being a goalkeeper? Is it fun?"

Tina was surprised, then remembered that Meg had probably asked Zoe to help Tina feel like part of the group. That had to be why Zoe was trying to talk to her.

"Well, I'm not a goalkeeper — not yet. But practice was okay."

"When did you start playing soccer?"

"I played on my first team when I was six. But my dad and I started kicking the ball around when I was three. He loves soccer."

Zoe smiled. "Really? That's awesome! *My* dad and my brother don't care about any sport but football. I mean, they go to my games, but I think it bores them. You're lucky."

Tina shrugged. "Well, my dad is from Argentina, and soccer is, like, the number one sport there. He played when he was younger, and he watches it all the time."

Zoe nodded. "Uh-huh. See, my dad was a football player in high school, and my older brother plays on the high school football team. So I'm the only one who cares about soccer at home. I don't think my brother even knows how many players are on a soccer team."

"That's too bad. I mean, Dad can be totally boring when he goes on and on about great Argentine soccer stars, but at least he *cares,* and he knows the game. My little brother is totally into baseball, though." Tina found that she was having no problem chatting with Zoe.

"*Yo, Maddy!* Does your mom know you're sitting here scarfing down junk food? Give me some of that pizza!"

A skinny redheaded boy had come racing up to the table.

The girl who had to be Maddy sneered up at the redhead. "Why don't you go play in the Kiddy Korner, Sean?"

Several other boys came along behind him in a noisy, laughing crowd. The girls knew and liked the boys, and a loud, teasing conversation began. Zoe was drawn in, and Meg, of course, was delighted with the new arrivals. Tina sat like a statue with an embarrassed smile on her face.

She was wondering if she could sneak away without being spotted, when she saw her neighbor, Dave, standing alone on the edge of the crowd, looking as unhappy as Tina felt. He saw Tina, and his face brightened. He waved. She smiled back, and he came over.

"Hi! How you doing?" she asked.

Dave looked back at the crowd of yelling, laughing kids. "Better since I saw you. These guys from my class asked me if I wanted to come here with them, and I said yes because I want new friends, but . . . I guess it takes time."

Tina sighed. "Tell me about it. I came because a girl on our team asked Meg and me. Well, *Meg* is having fun. But I'd rather be somewhere else."

"Boy, me too." Dave sat next to Tina and spoke quietly so only Tina could hear him. "I mean, I guess they're nice guys and all. But it takes me time to relax with people I don't know. I was happy to see you here."

"Really?" It was good to hear someone — especially a boy — say that her being here made him happy. "Me too. I mean, I'm not great in big groups like this, and I don't really know these people, either. Except Meg, that is. Oh, and Zoe, who's nice. But before I saw you I was thinking maybe I could just leave without anyone noticing."

Dave nodded, looking at the other kids. "Meg looks like she's enjoying herself."

Tina smiled and sighed. "Meg is amazing. She

always fits right in. I don't understand how she does that. I always freeze up. I wish I could be more like her."

"So, how's soccer going?" asked Dave.

"Pretty good, so far. Except it looks like I'm going to be the goalkeeper, or one of them."

Dave's eyes widened. "No kidding! Hey, great! Congratulations!"

Tina shrugged. "I don't know."

Dave looked surprised. "Wow. How could that be bad news?"

"It is if you don't want a spotlight on you," Tina explained. "Everyone watches the keeper. People cheer you one day and boo you the next, and I don't want either one. You even wear different colors from the rest of the team."

Dave nodded. "I guess I understand. But I still think it's a great chance for you. When you stand out on a team, you're automatically popular. Then you get used to people wanting to spend time with you. This is your chance!"

Tina stared at Dave. "If someone's a good athlete, they're popular even if they're boring? That doesn't make any sense!"

Dave shrugged. "Maybe, but it's true."

"But what if I do a *terrible* job as keeper? Then everyone will hate me!"

Dave thought for a moment before replying. "At my last school, we read this poem in English class. It was about a guy who was so afraid of being disappointed or of doing things wrong that he wound up never doing anything at all, ever. I think that's the worst thing that can happen to someone."

After a moment, Tina said, "So I should go to the mall and hang out with kids I don't really know or feel comfortable with because it's even worse to be alone and do nothing?"

Dave laughed. "Well . . . yeah, I guess."

"Uh, Tina?" Tina was so involved in talking to Dave that she was startled to see Zoe standing there with two other girls.

"Oh, hi. Uh . . . I . . . it's . . . ," Tina stammered. "Um, do you know Dave? Dave, this is Zoe. She's on our team."

Zoe and Dave exchanged hellos.

"I wanted you to meet my friends, Maddy and Lynn," Zoe said. "This is Tina. She's going to be a great goalkeeper. Tina, you saw Lynn at practice, she's a midfielder."

Tina remembered Lynn, though they hadn't talked.

"I'm glad you're going to be a keeper," Lynn said, looking like she meant it. "I wish we had you with the Wildcats last year."

Tina held up a hand. "I don't know how good I'll be, yet."

"If Danielle and Pepper say you can do it, I bet you can," Lynn replied. "Danielle's a good coach, don't you think?"

Tina was surprised that Lynn wanted her opinion. "Yeah, she's great. Pepper too."

A couple of other girls joined them, and suddenly Tina found herself part of a group of girls, talking about teachers, classes, and other stuff. Dave caught her eye and grinned. He mouthed the words "I told you so" and left to talk with other kids.

A while later, Meg came over and tapped Tina's arm. "I need to get home soon."

"Okay," said Tina, getting up. "We have to go," she said to Zoe. "See you next week."

"Bye, Tina, Meg," Zoe said. The other girls said

good-bye. Tina and Meg waved to Dave and got their bikes.

As they rode, Meg was in a great mood. "That was *great!* They're nice girls — *and* some of those boys too! Aren't you glad we went?"

Tina thought about it. She *was* glad, sort of. But something was still bothering her.

"Teen, come on! I saw you in that mall! You were talking to those girls, and they were talking to you! Admit it! You had fun!"

"It was nice," Tina admitted. "But . . ."

"But *what?*" Meg demanded. "Those girls liked you! Am I right or not?"

"*Did* they like me?" asked Tina. "Or were they just being nice because I'm a good athlete, or because you and Zoe asked them to?"

Meg stopped her bike with a squeal of brakes. Tina stopped to see what was wrong.

"Sometimes I do not *believe* you!" Meg stormed. "You're so sure you're boring that if people *do* talk to you then it has to be for some weird reason! They feel sorry for you or they think you'll be a soccer star or I asked them to be nice to you. Can't you just accept that people may really like you? Right now I can't see why, but they do! *I* usually like you! Maybe other people might, even if you were an awful soccer player!"

Tina was so surprised by Meg's outburst that she stood there with her mouth open. Then, realizing how silly she had sounded, she began to laugh. Finally, Meg joined in.

"Okay, I sounded dumb just now," Tina admitted. "You're right, I don't make sense sometimes. But that's how I feel, even if it sounds stupid."

She held her hand over her heart and gave Meg a solemn look. "I pledge to try to believe that kids might enjoy my company. Okay? I really will."

Meg glared at her friend. "Well, okay. Teen, you're not boring. But you *are* weird."

6

anielle? Can I talk to you a minute?"

Practice was about to begin, and Tina wanted to get this little conversation over before she changed her mind.

Danielle, who was writing on a clipboard, said, "Sure thing. What's up?"

"About goalkeeping," Tina said. "I decided I want to. I mean, I'll be the Wildcat goalkeeper, or one of them. If you want."

Danielle said, "I'm glad to hear it. You and Andrea will both get plenty of playing time, I promise you. It's time to get started." The coach clapped her hands loudly and called out, "Listen up, everyone! Over here, please!"

The players, who had been stretching, chatting,

and checking their gear, gathered in a group around Danielle and Pepper.

"Today, after we finish our drills, we'll be doing some scrimmages," said Danielle. "We'll begin with short-sided ones, four-on-four, and we'll move on to nine-on-nine, which is the most we can do since we only have eighteen players. But we don't have a great deal of time before we begin playing games, so we need to work on game strategies.

"We'll also practice corner kicks, throw-ins, free kicks, and other special situations. For now, we'll split into two groups for drills. The following players will work with me, and the others with Pepper."

Tina was in Pepper's group, along with Zoe and Cindy. One of the things Tina liked best about her coaches was that they had so many different drills for basic skills such as dribbling and passing. Because of the variety, what might have been a monotonous activity remained fresh and interesting.

For example, today's drills included one in which the players and Pepper formed a circle twenty yards wide. Every other player had a ball. When Pepper blew her whistle, those with balls had to dribble across the circle and pass to the opposite player, who would then do the same. As they dribbled, players had to watch out for each other, so they couldn't watch their feet. Tina was an experienced player, but even she had some problems avoiding teammates coming at her from the side.

In another drill, the girls paired off and took turns dribbling, keeping the other player from stealing the ball by screening her off with her body and making more use of the outside edges of the feet in moving the ball.

Tina was paired with Cindy. Cindy had quick feet and had no trouble controlling the ball no matter what Tina did. When they switched, Cindy flicked the ball away from Tina with a lightning move. A moment later, she did it again. Tina couldn't see how and wanted to ask her. But as soon as the drill ended, Cindy turned and walked away without a word.

Tina walked over to Zoe. "Is Cindy mad at me? I've never even talked to her."

Zoe shook her head. "No, that's just how she is. Last summer she went to soccer camp, and now she thinks she should be a star. Anyone who's any good is a threat to her. You're a threat because you're good and the coach paid attention to you."

"Danielle doesn't want stars," said Tina.

Zoe shrugged. "Cindy wants to be one anyway. Lynn asked Cindy how she did some move, and Cindy wouldn't tell her."

Tina noticed Cindy with two other players. "Well, she talks to *some* people."

"Maybe they're not good enough to be a threat to her," Zoe replied.

Tina was puzzled. Cindy's attitude went against what Tina thought soccer was all about.

After the break, the coaches set up two four-on-four scrimmages. Using cones, they outlined two half-sized soccer fields, each with a single half-width goal. Two teams of four played on both fields, and the ninth player of each group was the goalkeeper for both teams. Every two minutes, the keeper would switch positions with one of the other players.

Tina was happy not to be in the goal for this scrimmage. Her team included Zoe, and Cindy was on the opposing side. Tina knew that Zoe was a better shooter than she was. When their side had the ball, Tina decided to set Zoe up. Taking a pass from another teammate, Tina dribbled toward the goal, hoping to draw players toward her and leave Zoe open. Sure enough, the defender who was marking, or guarding, Zoe moved in to block Tina's shot. But Tina faked the shot and passed to Zoe on the left wing. Zoe's low, hard shot went past the keeper's dive for a goal.

"*Great* defense!" sneered Cindy, and the girl who had been marking Zoe turned red from embarrassment. A minute later, Cindy, on offense, tried to dribble in for a shot, but Tina slid in front of her and knocked the ball away with her left foot. As Tina got up, Cindy glared at her but said nothing. The play had been perfectly legal.

For the rest of the scrimmage, Cindy saw to it that she stayed in Tina's shadow, so Tina's teammates had trouble getting her the ball. When Tina did get it, Cindy was all over her. Then, Zoe intercepted a pass and caught Cindy by surprise. Tina raced toward the goal and Zoe passed the ball perfectly, setting Tina up for a shot.

Before Tina could shoot, Cindy dived in from the side in a tackle that cut Tina's legs out from under her. She fell, and the ball squirted loose. Pepper blew her whistle to stop play.

"Cindy, that's a foul! In a game, you'd get a yellow card for that tackle. Play the ball, not the player's legs!"

Tina got up, brushing away loose grass.

"You okay?" asked Zoe.

Tina nodded. "I'm fine."

Cindy neither asked Tina how she was nor apologized. As Zoe stared coldly at Cindy, Pepper called, "Okay, nobody's hurt, play on!"

At first, Tina felt an ache in her right leg, but it went away. Just before the scrimmage ended, Tina had the satisfaction of intercepting a pass meant for Cindy that would have left Cindy open for a shot. Once again, Cindy said nothing, but an ugly scowl appeared on her face.

As the scrimmage came to an end, Pepper beckoned to Cindy and talked to her quietly. Zoe and Tina watched. It was clear that Cindy didn't like what the coach was saying.

"What's with her?" Zoe asked.

Tina shrugged. She didn't have a clue.

While Danielle took the rest of the team to work on corner kicks, Pepper went off with Tina and Andrea for some goalkeeping drills.

To start, they did the drill in which they lay on their backs, threw balls in the air, and jumped up to try to catch them before they hit the ground. Tina had worked on this at home and was able to get to her feet more quickly. Andrea was still having trouble.

After watching the other girl for a moment, Tina said, "Try rolling to the side and pushing yourself up with a hand."

Andrea did what Tina suggested and found that she could scramble up more quickly. She grinned at Tina. "Hey, thanks."

The two keepers then spent time throwing or rolling "shots" for the other one to catch or block. When Tina dived to her right to trap a ball, she found that her leg was still a little sore. But she played on, realizing that the problem wasn't serious.

For the last part of the practice, the team split into squads of nine for a full-field scrimmage. Tina and Andrea were the keepers, as they would be in regular games. Cindy and Meg were on Tina's squad, and Cindy was a midfielder.

A minute into the scrimmage, Tina was faced with a scoring threat as Zoe, Lynn, and another girl moved into position for a shot. Tina started out of the goal to try to cut down their shooting angle, but as she did, Cindy darted in front of her, blocking her view of Lynn and the ball. Tina suddenly saw the ball, headed for the left corner of the goalmouth. She made a desperate lunge to the left and managed to punch the ball away. But Zoe controlled it and got off a second shot. This one was high, and Tina had to leap for it. She caught the ball overhead, brought it down, and rolled it out to Meg, who was unguarded in the backfield.

"*Hey!*" Cindy yelled. "I was right in front of you! That should have gone to me!"

Tina fought back the urge to yell, Well, you shouldn't have *been* in front of me! She knew that Danielle had to have seen what Cindy did, but Danielle didn't say a word.

As play went on, it appeared to Tina that Cindy had decided that Danielle approved of her behavior, because she kept on getting in Tina's way in front of the goal and yelling at Tina (and at other teammates as well) when they didn't pass the ball to her.

During a brief break in the action, Meg whispered to Tina, "That Cindy is such a creep! Why don't you talk to the coach about her?"

Tina was watching as Cindy talked to two other players. As she watched them, they all looked her way. Tina felt some of her old self-consciousness come back. Then she felt angry.

But she told Meg, "No, I don't think I should complain to Danielle. It'd look bad."

"If you want, I'll talk to her," Meg offered. "She shouldn't get away with that."

But Tina shook her head. "Danielle saw everything. If she doesn't want to say something to Cindy, there must be a reason."

"I think you should do something," Meg insisted. "She has to cut that stuff out!"

Tina said, "I'm not going to complain to Danielle, and I'm not going to do what Cindy's doing and make more problems for the team. And I don't want you to do it for me. Okay?"

Meg wasn't happy, but she agreed.

After the scrimmage, Danielle called the Wildcats together. "That was very good, for our first full scrimmage. We don't have a lot of time before the real games begin, but we're making progress. Everybody, work on your skills at home whenever you can: dribbling, passing, shooting. See you tomorrow!"

As the players broke up, Danielle signaled to Tina and Andrea to come over. "Pepper says you're both doing well as goalkeepers. I just wanted to mention that you can pick out the uniforms you'll wear in games. You can make them anything but sky blue and gold; that's what the rest of the team will wear.

"Andrea, do you have anything to say, any questions?"

Andrea smiled. "No, everything's fine."

Danielle looked at Tina. "How about you? Anything to say?"

Tina sensed that this was her chance to say something about Cindy. She thought about it for a moment and finally shook her head.

"All right, then," Danielle said. "Work on those drills! Bye!"

As she changed into her regular shoes, Tina

decided that she was right not to complain. Some-how, sometime, she'd have to figure out a way of dealing with Cindy if Cindy continued to act up.

But taking it to the coach — that was definitely not the way to go about it.

7

After school the next day, Tina was in her room and heard the thump of a soccer ball being kicked. She looked out the window and saw Dave kicking a ball against his garage wall. She opened her window and stuck her head out.

"Hi!" she called. "What's up?"

Dave smiled up at her. "I'm going to play with a team! Practice starts in a couple of days, and I need some work."

"Want company?" Tina offered.

"Great!" Dave said. "Come on!"

Tina ran outside. For a while they passed the ball back and forth. They took turns making high throws so that the other one could head it back. Dave was better at it than Tina was.

"Keep your neck and upper body rigid when you

head the ball," Dave said. "When you move, bend from the waist. Throw it to me head-high." Dave showed Tina what he meant. Then he tossed it back for Tina to try.

"That's better," he said, after she did it. "Try to hit the ball with the middle of your forehead, not the top. And keep your eyes open."

As they practiced, Meg showed up.

"Hi, guys," she said. "Can I play too?"

Tina said, "Let's go to the park. Maybe you two can help me with my goalkeeping."

At the park, they used their jackets to mark off a goal. Dave and Meg kicked shots, which Tina tried to block, and usually did.

After she sprang to one side and scooped up a hard shot, Dave said, "Hey, you're good!"

Tina smiled. "Thanks. Throw me more shots I have to jump for."

They lobbed balls that Tina had to leap to catch or to punch over where the crossbar of the goal would be. They tried to put shots into the corners of the goal, so she had to dive to both sides. After ten minutes, Tina was panting but happy. She was getting a good workout.

The three passed and dribbled for a while, then sat down for a rest.

"Guess who I saw today," Meg said. "Cindy and her friends, talking. They saw me and shut up, like someone flipped a switch."

Tina frowned. "Why, do you think?"

"Because I'm your friend," said Meg. "They were probably talking about you."

"Who's Cindy?" Dave asked. "It doesn't sound like she's a buddy of yours."

Meg laughed. "Hardly. She wants to be the superstar of our team, and she hates it that someone else, like Tina, might be as valuable to the Wildcats as she thinks she is."

Dave frowned. "Is she making trouble?"

Tina described what Cindy had done.

"What did your coach do?" Dave asked.

Tina said, "Nothing, but she must have had a reason. She's a great coach, and I can't believe she didn't notice what was going on, or that she didn't care."

Dave leaned forward and looked hard at Tina. "If the coach doesn't do something, you have to. If you let her get away with that stuff, she'll keep pushing you until you push back. You have to show you won't take it."

"I won't fight!" Tina didn't like Dave's suggestion. "I hope she'll lighten up, but I'm not going to make things worse than they are!"

"I'm not talking about fighting. The thing is," Dave said, "sometimes you just tell someone to back off. A guy at my old school gave me problems like yours. He came on like he was the Big Boss. One day he got in my face with a lot of loud talk, and I came right back at him. Well, he backed down and left me alone."

Tina said, "What if he hadn't? I'll do something, if Cindy keeps it up."

"What'll you do?" asked Meg.

Tina shook her head. "I don't know. But I will. When the right time comes."

"Well, I'll be there to help," Meg said. "And if you want me to talk to Cindy —"

Tina shook her head. "No. I have to do it, whatever it is. I don't want to start some kind of war on the team where everyone takes sides. I'd better go home and get ready for dinner."

They walked back to Tina's, where Dave waved and ran up the steps and in his front door. As Meg unlocked her bike, she said, "So you like Dave after all, huh?"

"Sure," said Tina. "He's a nice guy. Plus, he gave me some soccer tips."

Meg nodded. "Yes, but I mean, you *like* him. *You* know what I mean."

Tina said, "I think he's a friend, like you, except he's a boy. Okay?"

Meg gave up and left. Tina, who knew what Meg meant, was happy to drop the subject.

As Mr. Esparza served Tina some grilled beef — he was a good cook and often made the family dinner — he asked, "So what's happening with your team? Are you still a goalkeeper?"

Tina took her plate. "Thanks, Daddy, it looks delicious! So far, that's still the plan. I'm doing keeper drills with another girl and the assistant coach, and it's going all right."

A thought struck her. "Dad, you were playing soccer when you were my age, right?"

"Sure!" said her father as he served Sammy. "We played everywhere — in the park, in empty lots, in the street."

"Did you ever have a problem with a pushy kid who thought he was a star, hogged the ball, and gave you trouble all the time?"

Mr. Esparza gave his daughter a long look. "Yeah, we had a few like that. There are always a few like that."

Tina asked, "How did you handle it?"

"It depended. There was this boy who thought he was better than the rest of us and said so. The thing is, he *was* better, and we knew it, so we left him alone. He wasn't around long. Soon he went to a junior pro team, and in a few years, he was a real star.

"But most of these types aren't as good as they think they are. We didn't do much about them, either. It soon became clear that they weren't so good. They'd see it themselves and quiet down. Or they'd see they weren't making friends with all their talk, and they'd stop or go away and find other people to bother."

Tina wasn't sure this helped her or not. Cindy *was*

78

pretty good. "So, you wouldn't stand up to the person and tell him to, like, cut it out?"

"That's what *I'd* do," said Sammy.

But Mr. Esparza shook his head. "Maybe in a street game, where we chose sides, there might be arguing or even a fight. But on a real team like yours? No. A coach can take a loudmouth aside and tell him to stop, to be a team player. But one teammate doesn't fight another one. It makes for bad feelings, and if it happens, both players are to blame."

Mr. Esparza looked at Tina for a moment. "If I knew someone who had that kind of trouble, I'd tell him — or her — relax, don't get excited. Things have a way of working out."

"Thanks, Daddy." Tina felt better. She decided that by doing nothing, she'd been doing the right thing.

Over the next few practices, things stayed about the same with Cindy. She didn't talk to Tina except to yell at her now and then for not getting her the ball or for something else Cindy didn't like. Tina kept quiet, and as far as she knew, Danielle said nothing to Cindy.

Pepper continued to work with Tina and Andrea. In addition to drilling the girls on catching, blocking, and other skills, Pepper spent time talking about goalkeeping strategy.

She'd say, "When an opponent wants to shoot, make her shot harder by coming out of the goal and giving her a smaller target. If you're right in the goalmouth, the shooter has almost the whole eight-yard cage to shoot at. But if you move in, she has to shoot around you. *But* don't get caught out of the goal, in case a ball gets loose. You'll give up an easy shot."

Andrea sighed. "It's complicated."

Pepper grinned. "You bet. But that's what makes it a challenge. Here's something else to think about. Let's say you stop a shot and have the ball in your hands. What do you do with it? There are different ways to distribute the ball.

"If you're a strong, accurate kicker who can kick to midfield, and if you have a forward who can head the ball and control it, a long kick is a great way to start an offensive drive. *If* you can kick it to where you want it to go.

"You can throw to a defender or midfielder — if you can throw long overhand and control the ball, that is. Always throw to the side, not in front of the goal.

"The surest way to go is to roll the ball to a teammate, especially a good dribbler. But be sure she's looking and sees the ball coming.

"Or you can dribble the ball yourself and move it up before getting it to a teammate. But that's dangerous. If an opponent takes it away, the goal is unguarded.

"Spend time on your kicks and throws. See what you're good at and where you need work. If you're not sure where the ball will go if you kick it, don't kick. Any questions?"

Tina asked, "Does the keeper always decide what to do and who to get the ball to?"

"Definitely," Pepper said. "On defense, the keeper is like the team general. *You* decide, and don't let anyone else tell you what to do. That's important. When the other team has the ball, the goalkeeper is in charge. You direct traffic. If you want a player out of your way, let her know. And she has to do what you tell her."

Tina nodded. Ordering people around wasn't something that felt natural to her. Could she do it? It seemed that she would have to.

At the next practice, Danielle reminded the team that they had only three more sessions before their first game of the year.

"From now on, we'll drill and scrimmage as a team. After the drills today, we'll play nine-on-nine. I'll be watching, and Pepper will be referee. Ms. Allen, Zoe's mother, will be the second official. She's played the game and knows the rules. But first, let's do our drills. Andrea, Tina, you'll work with Pepper."

Pepper took Andrea and Tina aside. "Let's see how your kicking and throwing are."

Tina's first kick was straight, but short. She sighed and waited for Pepper's reaction.

"Pretty good, for starters. Hold the ball longer instead of tossing it up before you kick," said Pepper. "And step into the kick more, so you bring your kicking leg back farther. You also want more follow-through after the kick."

Tina's later kicks were much better. She'd have no trouble kicking to midfield.

Andrea, however, kept kicking the ball off the side of her foot and out-of-bounds.

"Don't worry, you'll get better," Pepper told her. "But for now, I'd probably avoid kicking the ball in a game."

Throwing the ball was a different matter. Andrea's long fingers helped her control the ball, and her long arm gave her throws good distance. Tina's overhand throws went all over the place; twice the ball dropped down from her hand. Her throws were short, and her aim wasn't good.

"Well, we learned some things," Pepper said when they finished. "We know that Tina can use her kicking to move the ball in the right direction but that throwing is a gamble, for now. Andrea, you throw well, but you need work on kicking. That's helpful!"

"Put us together and we'd make the perfect keeper!" Tina said. Both Andrea and Pepper laughed. Tina realized, to her surprise, that she'd made a joke without worrying if others would think it was funny. She grinned.

The two girls did other drills while the rest of them worked with Danielle. Then Danielle called the team together again.

"We'll take a break and then begin our scrimmage. Everyone, take five minutes."

"You know what amazes me?" Meg said to Tina and Zoe as they sat in the grass. "I don't think we've ever repeated a passing drill or a dribbling drill since we first started practicing."

"You're right," said Zoe. "It's like they have this endless list of exercises."

"It never gets dull, for sure," Meg agreed. "Hey, is that Cindy's mom with her?"

Tina saw a tall woman in an expensive-looking

warm-up suit talking to Cindy. The woman was pointing and gesturing, and Cindy kept nodding. She didn't look happy.

"Yeah," Zoe said. "That's her. She's the one who wanted Cindy to go to soccer camp. Looks like she's giving Cindy instructions."

Meg nodded. "Cindy doesn't like it."

Tina watched mother and daughter and said, "I bet if Danielle sees, she won't like it either."

"You're right," said Zoe. "Coaches don't like parents to coach their own kids — or anybody else's kids."

"I don't blame Cindy for not liking it," said Meg. "I'd hate for my mom to do that."

Danielle divided the team into squads. Tina and Andrea were the goalkeepers. Tina's squad included Cindy and Zoe, and Meg was on the other side. From her position in front of the goal, Tina had a good view of the action.

Cindy was definitely fast, and her quick feet helped her steal the ball from opponents — as Tina already knew. But Cindy did too much on her own. She'd try to dribble through a whole team and shoot. The first time she did that, Zoe was open, in perfect position for a shot from the left wing. Cindy ignored her and took a long shot herself that Andrea had plenty of time to grab.

From the sidelines, Mrs. Vane yelled, "Cindy! Get closer!"

Andrea threw to Meg on her left, who passed off to a midfield teammate. Cindy darted over to try for a steal, but the girl screened her off and passed to a wing. The wing and another forward moved in on Tina, who braced for a shot. The forward on Tina's right passed across the goalmouth, and Tina advanced toward the other girl, who wanted to shoot. The girl tried to chip the ball over Tina's head, but Tina backed up and stretched, arms high. She punched the ball over the crossbar and out-of-bounds, setting up a corner kick for the other team.

Cindy trotted by the penalty box and muttered, "You should have caught the ball," so that only Tina and a few others could hear. Tina turned red, but didn't say a word.

The corner kick came across the penalty box. The center forward headed the ball to the left wing, who dribbled closer to Tina. As Tina was trying to see where a shot might come from, Cindy raced in front of her, blocking Tina's view. As Cindy slid to the grass in an attempt to tackle the wing and steal the ball, the wing passed back to the center forward, who got off a lightning-fast shot. Tina lost sight of the ball for only a few seconds, but that was enough. She saw the shot coming too late and tried to get to it, but it was by her for a goal.

Tina's impulse was to scream at Cindy, but she didn't. Partly it was because she hated to make a fuss. Also, after seeing Cindy's mom in action, Tina thought she understood what made Cindy do the stuff she did.

As Pepper took the ball to resume play, Tina noticed Danielle walk over to Mrs. Vane and speak to her. She couldn't hear what was said, but it was clear that Mrs. Vane didn't like it. After a short discussion, Mrs. Vane walked away, looking angry.

When play started again, Cindy made a nice goal, heading the ball in on a pass from Zoe. Cindy glanced over at her mother, who nodded but didn't smile. Each team had scored a goal. A minute later, Meg made a quick move to intercept a pass. Cindy, who had been looking for another shot, was out of position to defend, so Meg had a long, open pass to a teammate at midfield. Suddenly, Tina was facing another scoring threat.

A couple of Tina's squadmates tried to get back to help, but one of the opposing forwards made a nice crossing pass to her teammate, who faked a shot to the left side, pulling Tina in that direction. She then slammed the ball past Tina into the right side of the cage for a goal.

"Really nice job!" yelled Cindy, pulling up short in front of Tina. "Why were you out of position?"

"Why was *I* out of position?" Tina yelled. "If *you'd* been in position instead of all over the field, they would have never gotten a shot at all!"

Immediately, Tina felt awful. The words had popped out of her mouth before she knew it. Cindy turned on her heel and stormed to her starting position. Zoe trotted over, seeing how upset Tina was.

"It's okay," she said. "You're totally right; she's trying to be a one-woman team."

"I shouldn't have yelled," Tina muttered, staring at the ground.

Zoe patted Tina's shoulder. "Well . . . no, but Cindy shouldn't have, either. It's cool. Really."

Play resumed, and a minute later, Tina made a

nice save, stretching herself full length in the air to get a hand on the ball and send it out-of-bounds. Meg made the corner kick, which came rocketing toward the goal. Tina got a hand on it and drew the ball into her belly, cradling it with both arms. Seeing Cindy sprinting toward midfield, Tina kicked it in her direction. Cindy headed the ball and dropped it at her feet. For once, she passed off — to Zoe, who dribbled toward the opposing goal and then passed back to Cindy. Cindy tried to kick a goal from forty feet away — too far again, giving Andrea time to catch the ball. When Danielle ended the scrimmage with her whistle, Meg's team still led, two goals to one.

As the Wildcats grouped around the coaches, Meg whispered to Tina, "You looked good."

Tina shook her head. "I wasn't that good. You guys beat us."

"You stopped more shots than Andrea," Meg replied. "And we wouldn't have scored the first goal if Cindy hadn't been in your way."

Before Tina could say anything more, Danielle called out. "Listen up, everyone. It went pretty well. I saw a lot of good play and hustle today. There are a few things we need to watch out for, though."

Danielle mentioned problems she had noticed: players being out of position, not passing to open teammates, and so on. She didn't mention names, but twice, Meg glanced at Tina and silently mouthed, "Cindy."

"Finally," Danielle said, "we have to remember that we're a team. That means there's never any place for anger or yelling. Teammates support each other. Arguing hurts the team. I hope I won't have to bring this up again."

Tina knew that this was aimed at her, at least partly. As she unlaced her soccer shoes, Meg nudged her and pointed. Tina saw Danielle talking to Cindy, who was red-faced.

"I knew the coach wouldn't let Cindy get away with that stuff," Meg said.

As Cindy walked away from the coach, Danielle beckoned to Tina.

"Now it's my turn," sighed Tina.

Before Danielle spoke, Tina said, "I'm sorry I yelled. I won't do it again."

"That's all right," said the coach. "I'm sure you won't lose your temper. But there are times when it's not only okay for you to raise your voice to teammates — it's necessary. You need to start doing that when it's called for."

Tina was startled.

"Pepper talked to you and Andrea about goal-keepers being field generals," Danielle went on. "That means, when a player is blocking your view in the penalty area, or when you want a player to move so you can pass her the ball or for any other reason, you have to tell her. You have to tell her loud enough to be heard. That isn't yelling because you're angry, that's part of a keeper's game. Don't be afraid to do your job, okay?"

"Okay," Tina said. She knew it was something she would have to work on.

Later on, Tina and Meg sat on Meg's front porch. "It was good to see Danielle talk to Cindy," Meg said. "She deserved it."

Tina curled her legs under her on the porch chair. "I never though I'd say this, but I feel bad for Cindy, now."

Meg stared at her friend, then laughed. "You're amazing! After what happened today?"

"Yeah, but Cindy's mom must give her a lot of grief," Tina replied. "Cindy must feel that if she isn't a star, her mom will be all over her. With most of us, if we do well, fine, and if we don't do well, it's too bad but it's no big deal. If Cindy doesn't do well, it *is* a big deal. I think she's afraid not to be a star."

Meg was quiet for a minute. "I guess," she finally said. "What did Danielle tell you?"

Tina smiled. "She says I *have* to yell more — it's part of what goalkeepers do. They have to let players know they're out of position, move them around. So, yelling can be a bad thing, or it can be a good thing, and I have to figure out which is which. Soccer is complicated sometimes."

Meg smiled. "*Life* is complicated sometimes."

"That's the truth," said Tina.

9

Tina was doing some stretches while waiting for practice to begin the next day, when she heard someone say, "I'm sorry I yelled at you yesterday."

Startled, Tina looked up to find Cindy standing in front of her, looking grim, as if she were doing something she really disliked.

For a moment, Tina was stuck for a reply. Cindy waited a moment, then turned and began to walk away.

"Wait!" Tina called, and ran after her. She got in front of Cindy, who stopped and looked at her, unsmiling.

"I'm sorry I didn't say anything just now, it's just that I . . . anyway, I'm sorry too. For yelling. I mean. It won't happen again."

"Okay," Cindy said, without a smile. Tina was sure that Cindy hadn't apologized because she felt she'd been wrong, but because she'd been told to.

"You know," Tina said, "I —" She stopped just before blurting something out about how rough it must be for Cindy to deal with her mother's demands. She suddenly realized that this would be a bad idea. Once again, she stood there without knowing what to say next.

Finally, Cindy shook her head and left.

"What did *she* want?" asked Meg, who had arrived just in time to see Cindy and Tina together.

"She apologized for yelling," Tina explained.

"Huh," Meg said. "She didn't look really sorry, did she?"

The girls heard the sound of a whistle. "Gather round, everyone!" called Danielle.

Once the team was together, the coach said, "Our first game, against the Rockets, is in two days, so let's make good use of our time. We'll start with drills. Tina, Andrea, work with Pepper. Everyone else, stay here with me."

While most of the team practiced passes, shooting,

free kicks, corner kicks, and other skills, Tina and Andrea worked on goalkeeping. During the workout, Tina saw that her throwing hadn't improved, but at least it wasn't any worse. Her hands, she thought, were too small to control the ball, but she could kick it a long way. Andrea's kicking was still not great, but her throwing was excellent. The girls spent time throwing and kicking shots for the other to block or catch.

"I wish I could kick like you do," Andrea said at one point. "That makes a big difference. "I'm not coordinated enough."

Tina smiled. "I wish I could throw like *you* do. Sounds like we're even."

After drills, before the team split up for a scrimmage, Danielle said, "Here is the starting lineup against the Rockets. Now, remember: Everyone will play. And I don't mean just for a minute or two. Everyone will get a *lot* of playing time. That's because you'll all need rest and also because everyone is working hard and deserves to play. Any questions?"

There were no questions, and the coach named the starters. Tina would be the keeper, Cindy was left wing, and Zoe was midfielder. Meg would come in off the bench. This was no surprise; Meg had expected it and wasn't unhappy. She knew she wasn't a top player, and the coach had said everyone would play.

Once again, the team was divided into two squads of nine, with Pepper and Zoe's mom as referees. This time, Meg was Tina's teammate, while Cindy and Zoe were on the other side. Danielle told Tina and Andrea that they'd get to play a position other than keeper, for part of the time anyway, so that they'd stay in practice for other positions — just in case.

For the first ten minutes, nobody could score, as both Tina and Andrea stopped several shots. Cindy, whose mother did not show up, threatened to get to a loose ball directly in front of Tina's goal, but Tina sprinted out and scooped up the ball before Cindy could reach it. Tina rolled it to Meg, who dribbled it away from the cage, out of danger.

A few minutes later, Zoe, from midfield, dribbled through two defenders and passed to Cindy on the wing. Cindy made a clever side-step move to get past one defender, then passed to a teammate. She then moved within five yards of the goal and waited for a return pass. Trying to mark Cindy, Meg stepped directly in front of Tina, so that Tina lost sight of the ball.

"Meg, out of the box!" Tina called.

Meg was startled, but stepped away just in time for Tina to see the ball headed straight for where Cindy could head it. Tina rushed out to the edge of the penalty box and snatched the ball out of the air. If she'd left the box, she would have been penalized for using her hands; a keeper can only touch the ball with his or her hands while in the penalty box. This time, Tina kicked the ball long and hard, and one of her teammates managed to control it and send it toward the other goal.

"Sorry," Meg called to Tina as she ran after the action. Tina wondered if she'd be able to yell at someone who wasn't her best friend. She hoped so. A little later, when Cindy led another rush on the goal, Tina called out to another defensive player, signaling her to mark one of the forwards. The girl nodded and did what Tina wanted. But Cindy made a beautiful move to get past her defender and put a shot through the goal, just under the crossbar where it met the left upright. There was no way for Tina to stop it; the shot was perfectly placed.

Cindy's squadmates came up to exchange high- and low-fives. "Nice shot," Tina called out.

Cindy swung around and stared at Tina in surprise. "Excuse me?"

"I said, nice shot," Tina repeated. "It was perfect, no way I could get to it."

Cindy's mouth dropped open. She looked so astonished that Tina almost laughed. Finally, Cindy closed her mouth, nodded, mumbled something that might have been "Thanks," and walked away.

After a half hour of scrimmaging, both squads had allowed one goal. Tina thought she'd done a pretty good job and was happy that she seemed able to get players to move when she needed them to. Danielle ended play with a whistle. The players trotted toward her, and most of them sat down for a breather. They'd been playing hard and needed a break.

"Great hustle today!" Danielle said, clapping her hands and looking as pleased as she sounded. "We'll take a ten-minute rest and shuffle the squads around for a second session. Here are the new line-ups."

For the second scrimmage, Tina would be on the same squad with Cindy and Meg, while Zoe was an opponent. After naming the squads, Danielle said, "When we begin, I'd like Tina and Andrea to be midfielders, for a while anyway. "She named two other girls who would start as goalkeepers.

Once her breathing was normal, Meg turned to Tina and rolled her eyes. "Wow! I never ran so long in my whole life!"

Tina grinned. "It was rough, huh?"

Zoe, who had heard Meg's comment, said, "Sure it's rough, especially when you're not used to playing that long at a stretch."

"Right!" Meg agreed. "You keepers have it easy, standing there with your hands in your pockets most of the time."

"Want to switch?" Tina offered.

"No thanks," said Meg. "No way. But it's still rough, running around like that."

"First of all," Tina replied, "you won't be playing that long without breaks in real games. Second, you'll get used to it."

Meg shook her head. "Maybe, but it won't happen today."

When play started again, Tina was playing midfield. She quickly understood what Meg had been talking about. She hadn't been doing as much running as most of the team had, and she soon found herself breathing hard and sweating. For the first time, she realized that being a goalkeeper had its good points. She was an okay midfielder, Tina thought, but she might turn out to be a better-than-okay keeper.

A ball came her way from a squadmate. Tina dribbled and passed to Cindy, who pivoted to her right, screening the ball from the player marking her. Then she did something so fast that Tina wasn't sure what happened, except that Cindy had passed the defender behind and was racing toward the goal with another forward. I could practice forever and never move the ball as well as Cindy, Tina thought.

A few minutes later, Danielle called a time-out and moved Tina and Andrea back to their usual positions as keepers. Tina was relieved.

Shortly afterward, Cindy raced to try to get to a ball that had rolled into the penalty box near Tina. Tina, who was closing in on it herself, called out, "Mine!" almost before she was aware of it. Cindy slowed down to let Tina have the ball. As Tina looked over the field to see where she should release the ball, Cindy said, "Sorry."

Tina nodded, too busy to say anything, but she rolled the ball to Cindy so Cindy could move it out of danger.

A few minutes later, Meg made a bad pass that the other squad intercepted. Zoe passed the ball down-field to a wing, who avoided a defender and dribbled to within fifteen feet of the goal. She faked a shot with her left foot and drew Tina to her own right, and then let fly with a hard shot toward the other side of the cage.

Tina recognized the fake and shifted her weight back to her own left side. As the opposing forward fired the shot, Tina took two long steps to the left and flung herself toward the ball, stretching herself out in the air a foot off the ground. If the shooter had aimed for the corner of the cage, she would have scored a goal. But it wasn't far enough into the corner, allowing Tina to get a hand on the ball and deflect it to the right. The ball hit the upright, bounced away, and rolled out-of-bounds.

As Tina got up, she heard someone say, "Good save."

She looked behind her and saw that it was Cindy. "Thanks," she said, smiling. Cindy hesitated and then smiled back.

Hearing clapping from the sidelines, Tina saw Dave standing there. He waved and gave a thumbs-up sign. Tina also saw Cindy's mother, standing not far from Dave. She stared straight ahead, unsmiling.

When Cindy caught sight of her mom, her smile vanished. Tina, whose father had always been encouraging, felt sorry for Cindy, whose mom seemed anything but.

At the end of the second scrimmage, Pepper spoke briefly to Tina. "Very good. And I see you can be the general when you have to be."

Danielle then gave everyone her thoughts. "I know you all must be pretty wiped out today, but you need the work to be ready for the games. Remember, when you're on offense and you're off the ball — when you're not the one who has the ball — be careful not to let yourselves bunch too close together. It makes the defending team's job harder when you're spread out. And don't get in the keeper's way in the penalty area, it's the keeper's job to deal with it. Okay, everyone, good work, and we'll do it again tomorrow!"

Dave came out to talk to Tina, who was standing with Meg. "You made a couple of great saves! You two want to go to the mall?"

"I can't," Meg said. "I promised my mom I'd help her with some stuff at home."

"I'd like to go," Tina said.

"Great!" Dave answered. "Let's —"

"Tina? Can I talk to you?" It was Cindy, who looked unsure of how Tina would treat her.

But Tina was happy to be friendly if Cindy was. "Sure! Oh, this is my friend Dave."

Cindy smiled at Dave. "Hi. Um, I just wanted to say that . . . I'm glad we're on the same team. I think you're a great keeper and I . . . I'm sorry if I was mean before."

"That's okay," Tina said. "Hey, we're going to the mall, want to come?"

"I'd better ask my mom," Cindy said, and ran over to Mrs. Vane.

Dave asked, "Is that the one who gave you trouble?"

Tina nodded. "That's her. She seems different now."

Dave grinned. "You stood up to her, huh?"

"Well, no," Tina admitted. "But she stopped anyway."

After a short talk with her mother, Cindy walked over with a disappointed expression. "I can't go, too much homework."

"Maybe some other time," Tina said.

Cindy smiled. "Maybe. See you."

As they biked to the mall, Dave said, "Cindy kept looking at her mom during the scrimmage. What's the deal?"

Tina sighed. "Mrs. Vane wants Cindy to be a star, but I think Cindy just wants to be part of the team. I hope they work it out. Cindy's a good athlete, and I don't think she's happy."

At the mall, they headed for the Food Court. Tina, who really wanted a cold drink, saw a big group of kids sitting at some tables and suddenly felt panicked. She thought of turning away, but somebody called her name. With a sinking heart, Tina recognized Zoe.

"Hey, Tina, over here!"

Dave said, "Come on!"

Tina said, "Okay," but she knew it would end up just like it always did: with her stuck for things to say, looking dumb.

Here we go again, she thought.

10

It started the way it usually did, with Tina sitting like a statue and saying nothing. But Zoe leaned over and poked her arm. "Great save you made! That was an awesome move."

"What happened?" a girl asked, one whom Tina didn't know.

"Teen made this totally amazing dive," Zoe explained. "It looked for sure like the ball was going in, but suddenly she's, like, hanging in the air, and the ball is headed out-of-bounds."

The other girl looked at Tina with interest. "Yeah? How'd you do that?"

Tina shrugged. "I don't know, exactly."

"You don't know?" The girl gave Tina a look that said, You must be weird.

"It sounds funny," Tina said, "but when something

106

happens really fast in a sport, you don't think, you just do it. If you stop to think — it's too late. It's like your brain lets your body take over."

A boy who had overheard nodded. "I can see that. It's the same in baseball when you swing at a pitch."

The girl thought for a moment. "Sure, like when I dance, I don't think about how to move, it just happens."

Tina nodded. "Right. My brain shuts off sometimes in soccer." She grinned. "Too bad it also happens when I take science tests."

The kids who were listening laughed. Tina could hardly believe it. She'd made a joke, and it had gotten a laugh.

She had no idea how much time had passed when Dave said, "I have to go, it's getting late."

Tina was sorry to leave, but she stood up and said, "Well, see you" to the group, who waved and said their own good-byes.

"Hey, Teen," said Zoe. "You want to meet for lunch tomorrow? We go to the deli near school. Bring Meg with you!"

"Sounds great," Tina said. And it *did* sound great.

Riding home, Tina suddenly laughed.

"What's so funny?" Dave asked.

Tina shook her head. "Oh, nothing, really. It's just . . . I feel good, that's all."

"Me too," Dave replied. "That was fun. Hey, let's go again soon, okay?"

"Okay!" Tina agreed happily.

The two parted at their driveways. When Tina entered her kitchen, delicious food smells hit her nostrils. She suddenly realized that although she'd been in the Food Court at the mall, she hadn't eaten a thing. Now she was starving!

At dinner, Mrs. Esparza asked, "How long until your first game? It must be soon."

Tina said, "Two days. You'll all be there, right?"

"Right!" Mr. Esparza said. "Have you thought about what color you'll wear? It's your choice, isn't it? Since you're a goalkeeper."

"I was thinking red," Tina said, reaching for another biscuit. "Red is cool."

Sammy said, "Why do goaltenders —"

"Goal*keepers*," corrected his father.

"How come goal*keepers* wear different uniforms from everyone else?"

"So everyone can tell us apart from other players," Tina explained. "'Keepers always wear different colors."

Mr. Esparza gave his daughter a warm smile. "We'll get you a red outfit tomorrow. I feel good that you're a keeper. I'd like to have been a keeper myself."

"Daddy!" Tina exclaimed. "You always say you wish you'd been a center."

Her father shrugged. "I'd like to have been a great scorer *and* a star keeper."

Mrs. Esparza said, "Your father doesn't always make sense when he talks about *futbol*. We'll all be there for your game. Just don't expect me to understand what's going on."

"*I'll* be there, even though soccer is lame compared to baseball," said Sammy.

"How can my son say that?" asked Mr. Esparza, giving Sammy a mock scowl. "Maybe when you get older you'll be more sensible."

Mrs. Esparza laughed. "It didn't happen with you, dear."

At practice the next day — the day before the first game — Tina saw Meg, Zoe, and other girls with Cindy, who was demonstrating a new move.

"Start with the ball on your right foot," Cindy said as Zoe tried it. "Then step over the ball with that foot . . . that's it! Now shift your weight so the ball's under your left foot . . . *good!* Then use the outside of your left foot to dribble . . . you got it!"

Tina nudged Meg. "What's happening?"

Meg turned. "Oh, hi. Cindy's showing people a 'scissor move.' She says it's a great way to fake out a defender."

"Does it work?" Tina asked.

Meg looked exasperated. "Not for *me.* Zoe can do it, but when I tried, I tripped. Maybe if I try it in a game, the defender will laugh so hard that I'll get by her, and it'll work that way."

Tina giggled. "But it's good that Cindy's trying to help. She's turning over a new leaf."

"Maybe," Meg said. "Want to ask her? Here she comes."

Cindy was approaching, but before they could talk, Danielle called the team together.

"Okay, there's a lot to do today. Let's do some drills. Pepper will work with Tina and Andrea, and I'll work with the rest of you."

Pepper had the goalkeepers throw each other shots to catch or block, especially ones that the other had to dive or jump to reach. They worked on kicks and throws. Tina's throwing was more accurate than before — but the ball didn't travel any farther.

Danielle then divided the team into squads to work on corner kicks, direct and indirect free kicks, and penalty kicks. Tina and Andrea were goalkeepers for this part of the practice. Tina really enjoyed defending against direct penalty kicks, which are awarded to a team when an opponent commits an especially serious foul. In a direct penalty kick, it's one player against the goalkeeper. Tina found that it was a challenge she enjoyed, in a practice situation at least. How she'd feel in a game, especially if the game were on the line, she'd find out later.

During a break, Tina asked Cindy, "Where's your mom? Is she coming today?"

Cindy shook her head. "No, she isn't. I asked her not to come to practices anymore."

"Really?" Tina was impressed. It couldn't have been easy for Cindy to do that.

"Uh-huh," Cindy said. "We made a deal. She'll

111

come to games, but only to cheer. She can't tell me what I did wrong. Danielle's my coach. My mom's my mom."

The girls exchanged a smile.

Danielle split the team into squads. Zoe's mother was back to serve as a second referee and help Pepper, who was the lead ref.

"This is our last scrimmage before the real thing," said Danielle. "We'll make it as real as possible. Pepper will even hand out yellow and red cards — if anyone commits a serious foul. If you get a red card, you'll have to leave, and your squad will continue shorthanded."

When some of the players looked confused, Danielle explained. "Referees give players who commit serious fouls, such as unsportsmanlike conduct, yellow cards. Refs carry the cards with them, and when such a foul happens, they flash them near the player who made the foul. Yellow cards warn the player to behave. If the player then commits another serious foul, or a *very* serious foul, such as fighting, he or she gets a red card. Then the player has to leave the game and can't return. The player's team must finish the game with one less player than the opposition."

Tina had Meg on her squad, on defense, and Zoe as a midfielder. Cindy was on the other squad at center.

When play started, Cindy and the other forwards on her squad moved the ball toward Tina's goal. Meg tried to mark Cindy, who got around her with a dazzling fake, maybe the scissor move that Cindy had shown Zoe. Tina came out to cut down Cindy's shooting angle, but Cindy didn't shoot; she passed to the right wing. Zoe darted in and made a sliding tackle, skidding on the grass and poking the ball to Meg, who dribbled it away from the goal. She passed to Zoe, and the action moved away from Tina, who relaxed a little.

At the other end, Tina saw Andrea grab the ball off the ground, cradle it in her arms, and make a strong overhand throw to a defensive back. Neither squad could make a real attack for a few minutes, until Cindy picked off a pass and brought the ball back toward Tina. Tina braced herself for a possible shot. As Cindy and her squadmates moved closer, Tina shouted to Meg to move away from the cage. Cindy passed to her left wing, who returned the pass to Cindy. From forty feet away, Cindy fired a shot like a bullet on a line that would put it just over Tina's head. Tina shifted toward the speeding ball and caught it with her hands in the W-catch that Pepper had taught her.

Looking downfield, Tina decided that a long kick might be intercepted. She rolled the ball toward Meg, but an opponent got the ball first and tried a quick shot. Lunging, Tina punched the ball out-of-bounds, setting up a corner kick. As the other team got into position, Tina took a few deep breaths and turned toward the kicker. The corner kick went to Cindy. Cindy headed it across the goalmouth to the other forward, who hit a perfect volley — kicking the ball before it hit the ground — toward the corner of the goal. Tina fell forward and smothered the ball with her body, just before it crossed the goal line.

Tina saw Zoe open at midfield and kicked to her. Zoe passed to a squadmate, and seconds later, the girl kicked the ball into the cage. Andrea sprawled out, unable to reach it.

When the scrimmage ended, Tina's squad had just the one goal, but their opponents had none. Tina had blocked half a dozen shots and felt good about how she'd played.

As the team grouped around the coaches, several players sat on the ground while others bent over, hands on their knees, catching their breath. Tina's ribs felt a little achy from when she'd fallen on the ball, but she knew it was nothing to worry about.

"Very good, everyone!" Danielle said. "I think you should be proud of how you played today. We're as ready as we can be for tomorrow's game. I like the way you all gave yourselves plenty of space on offense — you didn't bunch together the way you've sometimes done in the past. And you were unselfish, you thought and worked *together*. Tomorrow, of course, I'll be bringing in substitutes whenever play is stopped for substitutions to be made. Nobody is going to play as long at a single stretch as you've been doing in these scrimmages. So don't worry about tiring yourselves out, and be ready to play with everything you have.

"Please be here no less than forty-five minutes before the game is due to start. Get plenty of sleep tonight and be sure to eat well tonight and tomorrow.

You're going to need all the energy you can store up. Thanks, and see you tomorrow!"

As the girls gathered their equipment together and left, Meg came up to Tina. "Want to get something to eat at the mall?"

"No," said Tina. "I think I just want to go home. I don't think I'm up for the mall today."

Meg frowned. "Are you worried about meeting a bunch of kids? Because we won't hang out with them, if you don't want to."

"It's not that," said Tina. "I'm just nervous about tomorrow."

Meg nodded. "Oh. Well, sure, I can understand that. I'll ride home with you, then."

There was almost no conversation as the two friends rode toward Tina's house. Tina was thinking about what the coach had said.

Get plenty of sleep.

Tina would get to bed early, that was certain.

She just didn't know whether she'd be able to sleep.

11

Bright sunshine woke Tina the next morning. Her first thought was: It's Saturday, there's no school. Then she saw her new red pants and jersey hanging from her closet door and remembered: Today was game day.

For a moment, Tina looked at the new goalkeeper's outfit. She had slept well, despite her worries the day before, and she felt fine. There was a light tap on her bedroom door.

"Sweetie?" her mother called softly. "Are you up yet?"

"Yes, Mom," Tina got out of bed.

"Okay, then, come down for breakfast."

"Great!" Tina realized she was starving. "Mom? Can I make myself bacon and eggs?"

"Sure," said Mrs. Esparza.

117

A few minutes later, Tina sat at the table, where Sammy was already gobbling a stack of pancakes, and picked up her juice.

"Good morning," she said.

"Morning, princess." Her father pushed away his plate and poured himself more coffee. "Did you sleep well? You got plenty of rest?"

Tina nodded and drained the juice glass. "Uh-huh. I feel really good."

"Hey, Teen, I made a sign to hold up at your game today," Sammy said. "Want to see?"

Without waiting for a reply, Sammy raced to his room. He came back holding a big piece of poster paper. It said "WILDCATS ARE THE BEST" in giant blue letters. Underneath was a drawing of an animal with huge teeth.

"That's neat, Sammy," Tina said. "Uh, is that a wildcat?"

"Yeah!" said her brother. "I made his teeth really sharp!"

Mrs. Esparza sat down with her plate and coffee cup. "We'll be cheering for you, sweetie. But your father will have to explain to me what's happening."

Mr. Esparza snorted. "She knows the game better

than she pretends." Then his face turned serious. "I'm proud of you, Tina. I know you'll do your best and play well. The great players of Argentina will be proud of you too."

"The most important thing," Tina said, "is knowing that my family will be there cheering for me. That's what matters."

The doorbell rang, and Sammy jumped up. "I'll get it!"

Mrs. Esparza smiled as she watched him race to the front door. "Your brother may say that soccer isn't as good as baseball, but he's as excited as the rest of us."

"I know," Tina replied, as Sammy came back, with Dave behind him.

"Hi," Dave said, "I hope it isn't too early to visit."

"Not at all," said Mr. Esparza. "Want something to eat?"

"No, I'm okay," Dave said. "I just want to wish Tina good luck. I'll be at the game."

"Great!" Tina said, beaming.

"We can take you with us, if you like," offered Mrs. Esparza. "Tina has to be there early, so she's going with Meg."

"Thanks, I'd like that," Dave said. "Well, I better go, see you later."

Tina said, "I'll walk you out."

"That's okay," said Dave.

Tina stood up. "No, I want to."

They went outside. Tina closed the front door and leaned against it. "How's your new team working out?"

"Really good, so far," Dave said, sitting on the front porch rail. The coach is cool, and I like the guys. I've made new friends. But you were the first friend I made here."

"I'm glad I'm your friend," said Tina. "I guess things are going well for both of us."

Dave asked, "Want to go to the mall for a victory celebration after the game today?"

Tina laughed. "Whoa! I don't know for sure that we'll have a victory to celebrate. Also, there'll be a team thing after the game. But if you want to come to that, that would be cool."

"Sure." Dave stood up. "Well, good luck, then. Go, Wildcats!"

"See you later," said Tina.

She finished her breakfast and went to her room

to put on her goalkeeper gear. Once it was on, she studied herself in the mirror. She liked the way the red outfit looked on her. Then she remembered how the thought of looking different from her team-mates, of standing out in any way, had been frightening to her. It hadn't been long ago, but now it seemed like ancient history.

Tina went downstairs and found the rest of the family still at the table. "I think I'll go over to Meg's and maybe do some stretching or something. I'm feeling a little nervous."

She hugged each member of her family. "See you later."

"We'll be there," said her father.

"You always are," said Tina, and she left for Meg's house.

12

As Mrs. Janis drove Meg and Tina to the soccer field, Meg was unusually quiet. She was wearing her blue-and-gold Wildcat uniform, and other than telling Tina that the red goalkeeper outfit looked good, she had nothing much to say. Tina, who was beginning to feel more and more nervous, realized that Meg was feeling the same thing.

The girls arrived at the field, which was freshly painted with lines, at the same time as a few other Wildcats. They saw Zoe talking with teammates and waved to them. Cindy got out of a car a moment later and ran over, while her mother watched from the car window. Danielle and Pepper stood a short distance away, going over some things on Danielle's clipboard.

As the Wildcats put on shin guards, checked shoes

and laces, and chatted, a bus pulled up. The Rockets filed out, wearing green and white. Danielle and Pepper greeted the Rocket coaches, and they talked for a few minutes. The officials — two women and a man, in black jerseys — joined the coaches. The first spectators drifted into the bleachers, and Tina spotted her family with Dave.

After the officials' conference broke up, Danielle called the team together.

"Hello, everyone! We've got a perfect day for soccer, so I hope we're all rested and ready. Just a few reminders: We'll play two thirty-five-minute halves. In the middle of each half, there will be a time-out for substitutions. Everyone will get to play.

"I think you're prepared for this game, and I know you'll give it your best effort. As long as you do that — play as a team, play hard, and follow the rules — then you'll be winners, no matter what the final score is. Pepper and I are proud of you. You already know who the starters are, so . . . go get 'em and good luck!"

There was a huddle of green and white at the far end of the field as the Rocket coaches gave last-minute instructions. Then, suddenly, it was game time. There was a sizable crowd in the stands, with rooters for both teams. The referee called the team captains to the center of the field for the coin toss. Winning the toss meant the team could either choose which goal they'd defend for the first half or whether they'd have possession of the ball to begin the game. Cindy came out for the Wildcats, who won the toss and elected to take the ball. That meant that the Rockets would have the ball to begin the second half. Both teams took their positions, and the referee put the ball down in front of Cindy and raised her arm. When she dropped it and blew her whistle, the game had begun.

Cindy kicked the ball back to Zoe, the Wildcats' best offensive midfielder, and the forwards moved into Rocket territory. At first, the Wildcats seemed to have an advantage, and the ball stayed mostly at the Rocket end of the field. Cindy managed to get off a hard shot, but the Rocket keeper grabbed it and sent the ball downfield with a long kick. Tina came alive, but the Rockets were unable to organize a real offensive threat. A Rocket forward did head the ball toward Tina at one point, but a Wildcat defensive player stopped it and started the ball back in the other direction. Tina never got to touch the ball in the first several minutes of play.

Cindy was playing very well, Tina thought, intercepting a few passes, preventing the Rockets from mounting any scoring threats, and keeping their defenders off balance with quick feet and deceptive moves.

But suddenly, a shout from the Rocket fans alerted Tina that some green-and-white jerseys were heading her way. The Wildcat defense struggled to get back into position. A Rocket midfielder had stolen the ball after a lazy pass, and the Wildcats had been caught off guard.

A speedy Rocket forward outran the Wildcat defenders and took a perfectly aimed pass to within ten yards of the Wildcat goal. Tina bounced on her toes, facing the ball, hands near her sides. As a teammate tried to get between the forward and the goal, the Rocket chipped a high pass across the field, where another girl in a green-and-white jersey timed her kick perfectly, and volleyed it to Tina's left side — at the corner of the cage!

Tina, who had advanced to her right, expecting a shot from the other forward, now took two quick steps to the left and dived to that side with both arms extended and her hands locked together. She was able to punch the ball away from the goalmouth, and it skittered out-of-bounds before another Rocket could reach it. The referee signaled for a Rocket corner kick.

Cindy darted back toward Tina and whispered, "Watch out for that redhead, she's going to try a header off the corner kick!"

Tina saw the redhead just beyond the penalty box on the right, and nodded. Sure enough, the corner kick came straight for the redheaded girl, who headed it toward the upper-left corner of the cage. But Tina had anticipated the move and leaped high to make a catch. At the same time, Cindy broke for the far end of the field. Tina rolled the ball to a back, who relayed it to Zoe. Three quick passes put the ball on Cindy's right foot. Cindy faked as if she were going to kick a goal and, with her other foot, passed to a wing. The Rocket keeper had been drawn out of position and tried desperately to get back, but the kick by the Wildcat forward was out of her reach and rolled into the net! The Wildcats led, 1–0.

A minute later, the referee signaled for a substitution time-out. Andrea came in for Tina, among several other replacements, including Meg, who came in as a defensive player. When play resumed, the Wildcats, with Cindy on the sideline, seemed a little disorganized, and the Rockets moved the ball into the Wildcat end of the field. Andrea stopped the first shot that came at her, scooping it up and quickly throwing it out to Meg. Meg tried to dribble the ball away from the goal, but she was tackled by a Rocket forward, and the ball was controlled by their center forward. The center made a nice back-pass to a midfielder who had come up. The midfielder fired a hard shot that Andrea couldn't see until it was too late. The tying shot was good, and Andrea lay stretched out full length on the grass. She started to get up, winced, and fell back down.

The referee stopped play, and Danielle and Pepper ran out to their player. A minute later, they helped Andrea up and supported her on both sides as she limped off the field. Andrea's face showed that she was in pain. The crowd stood up and applauded respectfully. While Pepper wrapped Andrea's leg in an ice-filled towel, Danielle came over to Tina.

"Andrea pulled a thigh muscle. It isn't serious, but

she can't play anymore today, so it's going to be up to you in goal. Think you can go the rest of the way yourself?"

Tina was stunned. *Could* she?

"I think so," she said, after a moment. "It's not like I have to run up and down all day."

Danielle smiled and said, "Try to pace yourself. I think you can do it, too."

Tina trotted over to Andrea, who was sitting on the bench with her leg stretched out. "How are you doing?"

Andrea sighed. "The ice kind of makes it numb. I'll be okay in a few days. Good luck!"

Tina ran onto the field to cheers from the crowd and her teammates. The referee gave the ball to the Wildcats to put into play, and the action began again.

Within a minute, the Rockets had taken the ball back from the Wildcats, and Tina found herself having to stop two more shots. After the second one, she kicked the ball to midfield and hoped that her teammates could hang onto it for a few minutes so she could catch her breath. As it happened, neither team was able to get any scoring opportunities before the first half ended in a 1–1 tie.

As Tina came off the field, panting, Cindy ran over. "You're doing great! Keep it up! We're going to win this game!"

Tina was too out of breath to do more than nod. Danielle clapped her hands to get the team grouped around her.

"All right, we suffered an injury, but we're right in the game! Remember, you're all wiped out right now, but so are they. In the second half, keep up the good work and try to help Tina out where you can. Don't block her view of the ball if you can help it. When she wants you to move somewhere, do it. Tina, if you make more of those downfield kicks, that might get our offense going more and tire out their defense. You're all doing well, so take a breather, and then let's go out and play a strong second half!"

Pepper squatted in front of Tina. "Watch out about getting too far away from the goal. That could be a problem."

Tina nodded.

Too soon for Tina's liking, it was time to start again. This half, it would be the Rockets putting the ball in play. At the whistle, the Rocket center toed the ball to her wing, who passed it back. The center advanced with the ball, and Tina came forward to cut down her shooting angle. The center passed to the side, but Zoe intercepted the pass and dribbled away from the goal. Watching the play, Tina was slow to retreat to the goalmouth again. Before she could react, a Rocket darted in front of Zoe and knocked the ball loose. Another Rocket took the ball, and before Tina could recover, fired it into the cage for a score. Tina dived but couldn't touch the ball. She lay on the ground, feeling awful: Pepper had just warned her about staying out of the goal, and she'd done it anyway!

"It's all right," said a voice. It was Cindy, kneeling in front of her. "We'll get it back! Don't let it get to you. Stay focused on the game! We need you right now!"

Slowly, Tina got to her feet and managed to smile at Cindy. "Thanks," she said. "I'm okay."

The Wildcats put the ball in play and moved it down the field, but failed to score. A few minutes later, Meg was penalized for getting in the way of the Rocket goalkeeper when the keeper was trying to pass the ball out of the penalty box. The Rockets were awarded an indirect kick. This meant that they were given a kick at the Wildcat goal from deep in Wildcat territory. The Wildcat players had to stay ten yards away from the ball until it was touched. Because it was an *indirect* kick and not a direct kick, two offensive players had to touch the ball before it could count as a score.

Meg was upset at the mistake she'd made. She had actually stumbled into the path of the Rocket goalkeeper, but it was still a foul, even if it was an accident. As Meg scowled at the ground, Tina came up to her.

"Don't worry — we'll get back into this game. Anyone could have done what you did. Don't beat yourself up over it."

The teams set up for the indirect kick. The first Rocket chipped the ball over the line of Wildcat defenders, and a second Rocket sprinted around the line to the ball. Tina came out and smothered the shot, falling on it and wrapping it in her arms. She jumped to her feet and rolled the ball to Meg, who was waiting to the left of the penalty box. Meg dribbled a few feet and saw Cindy open at midfield. She kicked a beautiful pass that Cindy took in full stride, racing down the middle of the field as the other Wildcat forwards caught up to her.

Cindy kicked the ball back to Zoe, a few yards behind her, and dashed forward toward the Rocket goal. Meanwhile, Zoe zipped a pass between two Rocket defenders to the Wildcat right wing. The wing volleyed the ball hard to Cindy, who was in great position for a shot. But before she could get the shot off, a Rocket tackled her, sliding into Cindy from behind and knocking her down. It was a serious enough foul to give Cindy a free direct kick.

As Tina watched from the far end of the field, the other Wildcats came up to give Cindy encouragement. Cindy nodded, waited a moment, dribbled once, faked left to draw the goalkeeper off, and fired a hard shot into the right corner of the goal net. The game was tied at two goals apiece. The Wildcats surrounded Cindy, hugging her and cheering.

During the last few minutes, Tina made one more stop, on a ball that curved to her left and forced her to dive to the side. Her uniform was now covered with grass and dirt stains. She kicked downfield, but before the Wildcats could do anything, the referee's whistle signaled the end of the game — a 2–2 tie.

Players from both teams came out to the middle of the field and shook hands. The game had been hard-fought, and Tina knew that neither team had anything to feel ashamed about.

As she walked slowly to the sidelines, she felt tired but happy. Danielle and Pepper took turns hugging her, as they did every Wildcat in turn. Danielle got everyone's attention with a shrill whistle.

"Great game! You should all be proud of your-selves. I'm taking Andrea to get her leg wrapped, and then I'm buying pizza for everyone, at Marco's in one hour!"

Tina nudged Meg and said, "I could use some pizza. How about you?"

Meg looked upset. "That stupid mistake I made cost us a good chance for a goal. We might have won."

"Hey, stop that!" Tina put an arm around her friend. "You played really well."

Cindy grabbed Meg's hand. "Hey, you started the play that set up the tying score!"

Meg's face brightened. "I did, didn't I?"

Tina saw her family coming and ran over to them.

"You were great!" yelled Sammy. "Did you see me with my sign?"

"I sure did," said Tina, exchanging a high-five with her brother.

Mr. Esparza put his hands on Tina's shoulders. "You played like an Argentine."

Tina hugged him. "Thanks, Daddy."

Mrs. Esparza said, "I thought that call on Meg was wrong. She didn't run into the goalkeeper on purpose. It should have been a simple throw-in for the other team."

"I thought you knew nothing about soccer," Tina said.

Her mother shrugged. "Even someone who knows nothing can tell a bad call."

"Going for pizza, Teen?" Cindy asked. Tina was happy to see Cindy and her mother with their arms around each other's shoulders.

"Sure," she said. "We earned it."

Dave came up, smiling. "Way to go, Teen! Excellent game!"

Zoe and several other girls came up to congratulate Tina, and Tina turned a little red.

"Something wrong?" asked Dave. "You have a nice bunch of teammates."

"They are," Tina agreed. "I guess I'm still a little uncomfortable about compliments."

"You better get used to it," Dave said. "I bet you'll get more during the season."

Tina thought for a moment. "I guess I *am* getting used to it. And, you know what? It's really not so bad."

Matt Christopher

Kobe Bryant	*Tara Lipinski*
Terrell Davis	*Mark McGwire*
Julie Foudy	*Greg Maddux*
Jeff Gordon	*Hakeem Olajuwon*
Wayne Gretzky	*Alex Rodriguez*
Ken Griffey Jr.	*Briana Scurry*
Mia Hamm	*Sammy Sosa*
Tony Hawk	*Venus and Serena Williams*
Grant Hill	*Tiger Woods*
Derek Jeter	*Steve Young*
Randy Johnson	
Michael Jordan	

The #1
Sports Series
for Kids

Read them all!

All available in paperback from Little, Brown and Company